# OUTPLAYED

# LILA ROSE

*USA TODAY* BESTSELLING AUTHOR

*Outplayed* Copyright © 2019 by Lila Rose

Cover Design: Letitia Hasser
Cover Photograph: Wander Aguiar
Editing: Hot Tree Editing
Interior Design: Rogena Mitchell-Jones

*Outplayed* is a work of fiction. All names, characters, events and places found in this book are either from the author's imagination or used fictitiously. Any similarity to persons live or dead, actual events, locations, or organizations is entirely coincidental and not intended by the author.

First Edition

978-0-6484960-2-1

# DISCLAIMER

This novel could be read as a standalone since it's set back when Violet and Travis first made contact (in *Holding Out*: Zara and Talon's story), where years have passed since they dated at university.

# PROLOGUE

## TRAVIS

*W*hen I walked into my office at my new home, I didn't expect to see my five-year-old daughter sitting at my desk holding a photo frame. I'd thought she'd been in her room drawing, yet there she was studying the photo like it was a puzzle.

"Princess, what are you doing?" I asked, making my way over to her.

"Daddy, who's this lady?" She held up the frame as I got to her side. My heart jumped.

*Violet.*

Gently, I picked Izzy up, sat in her spot on my desk chair, and placed her on my lap. "Her name is Violet."

"Why do you have her picture?"

I tucked her hair behind her ear and kissed her temple. "She was the one woman I loved with my whole heart. Unfortunately, work got in the way and I lost the chance of my happy ever after."

She was quiet for a moment. "She's real pretty, Daddy."

"I know, princess."

After moving to Ballarat, I had hoped to see Violet. Ever since I moved out of the country to New York, I had regretted it.

Leaving her after university was the worst decision of my life, yet I wouldn't be the man I was now without those changes. I wouldn't have what I did. We'd both chosen different paths back then; mine had been in construction in Sydney and she'd stayed in Victoria.

Then an opportunity to work under a big-named company in New York won me over. That was where I met a friend and we went into business together. Violet and I had had a plan: get our careers sorted and then eventually find one another again. Only it didn't work out that way. The woman I had been dating fell pregnant, and everything changed from then on.

Shit, I was even dating someone now, but I couldn't stand the woman any longer. I'd met Pam six months ago in Sydney when Izzy and I were living there for a year on business. Pam and I connected because she was in the state working, but she originally came from Melbourne. She interested me enough to want more than just casual sex. Only time told me I'd made a mistake when she became money hungry.

I would have got rid of her sooner, if she hadn't followed me to Victoria to begin with. Though, instead of making me pick her or the change of location, she took the choice out of my hands and made the move herself... with the money I'd given her of course.

So I kept her around because I wasn't as cruel as people believed—unless they fucked me or mine over. Then I was, as my friend Link put it, downright scary.

Soon though, very soon, I would happily see Pam out of our lives. I'd been meaning to get rid of her for some time, but the move, business, and Izzy had kept me busy. Fuck, I hadn't even gotten off using her body in over four months. She'd tried, but I couldn't handle her touch. Another reason she had to go.

She'd been the only girlfriend to meet Izzy, which I regretted, but it was by accident. Not that Izzy knew Pam and I were seeing each other. I made sure my daughter understood Pam was only a friend. She wouldn't even be that for much longer.

Violet didn't know the man I was now, but I knew the woman she was, and she wasn't the only one who could find out about a person. I knew she owned her own PI business, had Ryan Warden, Chuck Stanley, and Butch Callington working for her. She was thirty-four, looked twenty-five, and lived alone in the city. She paid her taxes on time, went out on a couple of dates in the past three years but preferred to go to the gym or stay at home reading or watching TV. I even knew when her rubbish day was.

Why?

Because I had stayed away for a decade in the hope she would marry or get a boyfriend that stuck, but she didn't. Her career meant the most to her, and it was time for me to teach her there was more to life than working.

It was time to reclaim the woman who had always been mine.

# CHAPTER ONE

## VIOLET

*S*ome have said I have a temper. Others said they didn't see it; those people didn't actually know the real me. I knew I had a temper, which was why I took up being a private investigator. I wasn't a people person. I didn't want to work in a police station or as a detective because I wanted to be in charge. I didn't want to work alongside dickheads. This way, I got to pick the people who I wanted around me. At first, I weeded out the douches who thought being a PI was all fun and games. It took a couple of years, but finally, I had the best team with Warden and Chuck, who, unfortunately, was leaving me soon, so I hired Butch to replace him. And I knew he would fit in well.

"You've ruined my fucking life, you bitch," Mr Donahue yelled as he stood in front of my desk.

"Well then, maybe you should have kept your dick in your pants," I suggested.

Just as he started to lean over the desk, Butch strode over, grabbed Mr Donahue's arms and hauled him towards the door.

"Get your hands off me. I'll sue," he screamed. "You're dead. You're all dead."

Raising my voice, I called, "Thank you for the death threat. It's been recorded, and if anything happens, the police will know who to look for."

I caught Mr Donahue paling just before Butch forced him outside, pushing him away from the building. Butch came back in, a scowl on his face. "Do you get many of these jerks coming in?"

"Mainly the cheaters getting caught out, yes. They don't want to take responsibility. They need to blame someone, and it's usually us."

The front door opened again. We both looked, expecting it to be Mr Donahue. It wasn't. "What did I miss?" Zara, my secretary, asked.

"Another husband complaining about being found out."

"I'm always getting lunch when the action goes down," she complained, dropping a bag of takeaway onto my desk and handing one to Butch. He gave her a nod and went back to his desk. "Butch, you need to meet Chuck out at Stanberry's place in an hour. Vi, you have a meeting in an hour with the Gradins."

I groaned.

Zara laughed. "Tell me again why you hate these meetings? Ones where the client is going to praise you for your good work after finding their child, when the police couldn't, I'll hasten to add. Yet you'd rather hide under your desk so you don't have to face them."

"I'm not good with praise. I just want to do the job, succeed, and then get paid."

Zara rolled her eyes and snorted. Since getting to know her and her bubbly personality, she'd grown on me. So much so, I would do whatever necessary to have her back. Zara shook her head before returning to her desk at the front. She'd been with us for a couple of weeks. I'd been meaning to look for an assistant but hadn't had the chance, and then she'd walked in with her resumé. As soon as she became flustered and told me her last name, which was different to the one on her actual resumé, I'd known she had a past she wanted to escape from. After she'd left, I found out exactly who her husband was and guessed she was running from him and his shit. My guesses were usually right. I wasn't sure if he would come looking for her here, but I wanted to be close to help if needed.

There was also the fact she lived opposite my brother's motorcycle club compound and one of his businesses.

A brother I hadn't seen in many years because he'd stuck with the Hawks MC even when they'd dealt with illegal things such as guns, women, and drugs.

Even after Talon had taken over as president and cleaned the place up, we hadn't reached out to one another.

We were both stubborn.

In a way, I hoped having Zara work with me would somehow lead me back into my brother's life where it wouldn't look like I was the one giving in.

I made sure my life was above board. Talon also did, but without a doubt, I knew his life would be run by his rules, and not all of them would be completely legal.

We were so *very* fucking stubborn.

"Please, thank you again. I can't say it enough for you bringing Angela back to us," Mrs Monroe said, shaking my hand for the millionth time. At least I had her to the front door; I was so close to having her gone.

"I'm just glad she's home, Mrs Monroe." I felt sorry for Mrs

Monroe. Angela was a hormonal teen with a big-arse attitude to boot, and would probably disappear with her older boyfriend in the next few weeks. But I'd done my job, and I didn't have to do anything else. Yet, I still raised my concern. "She may do this again."

Mrs Monroe sighed and nodded. "I had that feeling also."

"She's not eighteen yet, Mrs Monroe. Means you can change things."

"I'm going to try."

"Keep my number in case, and if you fear she's going to run, call me. Free of charge of course."

Tears welled in her eyes. It was my time to retreat. I didn't do well with crying since I hardly did it myself. "Thank you for coming in, but Warden is calling me over."

Warden, hearing his name being called, raised his head and rolled his eyes. "Ah, yeah, I need help with something for a second." He knew the drill. If he saw me dealing with an emotional client, he had to be my distraction.

Mrs Monroe nodded and hugged my tense body. "Yes, yes. You must be busy. Thank you again."

"You're welcome." I smiled before turning and making my way over to Warden. Zara would fix the bill, so I had to make sure I looked busy until the coast was clear.

Warden pointed at something on his screen. I nodded. He whispered, "You know you're a woman too and this crying shit shouldn't scare you."

"Shut up." I hissed through my teeth and grinned down at him. As soon as I heard the door open and close, I looked over. Zara was already shaking her head at me.

"What?"

She rolled her eyes. "Nothing."

"Good, I'm going to skip out early. Warden, you good to lock up?"

"You know it."

"Thanks. Butch and Chuck won't show until tomorrow, hopefully with some news on their case."

I went to my desk and grabbed my keys and purse before starting for the door.

"You have a 9:00 a.m. meeting with a Mrs Bendale," Zara reminded me.

"I'll be sure to arrive early for it. Later, guys."

"Bye." Zara waved. Warden grunted.

As I drove home, I smiled. Business was good. Even when I had pricks like Mr Donahue showing, I was still happy with how things were going. I'd caught up on most of my paperwork, so it was a night of relaxing and enjoying the quiet.

At home, I turned on the living room light since it was nearly dark, then walked into the kitchen and did the same. After I called for a pizza, I showered, then dressed in leggings and a hoody before heading to the kitchen to grab a bottle of water. Bottle in hand, I made my way into the living room. The quiet of the place had started to get to me more and more recently. I picked up the remote and sat on the couch, turning on the TV. Reruns of *Friends* were on, so I left it on the channel and got comfortable.

I glanced around my living room. I wasn't a woman who wanted much, but I was in a place where I could buy anything I wanted. I just didn't need much in life.

And I was happy.

I was.

I had a great business, wonderful colleagues, a place of my own. I went out when I wanted, which wasn't often. I dated when I felt the need to, and again, it wasn't often.

I was happy with how my life was.

I wasn't missing anything.

I refused to think of the man who could have been on the

couch beside me, if only I had asked him to stay. But I didn't want to be the woman to make a man pick her over his career. Especially when I'd been just as ambitious as he'd been.

I refused to think of the loss I felt when he left.

I hid it even when we'd kept in contact for a while.

Weakness wasn't something I showed. I'd been weak after he'd left. Weak because I'd missed him with every breath I took.

But I wasn't thinking of him and how I knew he was living in Ballarat. I refused to know where he actually lived. That way, I wouldn't head on over to see what he looked like after all these years. I refused to think of my desire to run into him down the street.

Lives changed.

People changed.

I'd heard how he'd changed, so not knowing him these days was for the better.

I would push all those thoughts of him aside.

I didn't need anything more in life. I *was* happy, and I'd keep telling myself that every day.

Instead of thinking of anything else, I would enjoy my show, my pizza, and my night all on my own.

Jesus, was I pathetic?

Or just feeling lonely?

Whatever it was, I didn't like it.

*Still... I wonder what he's doing right now.*

Bloody hell, where did me not thinking of him go?

The doorbell chimed. If it wouldn't have been weird, I would have kissed the hell out of the pizza delivery person for dragging me from my depressing thoughts. Instead, I gave them a huge smile and retreated to the sofa, pizza in hand, to indulge in brain-numbing TV.

# CHAPTER TWO

## VIOLET

*I*t was late when my phone on my work desk rang a few weeks later. I was still in the office trying to catch up on paperwork. I glanced to the screen to see Zara's home number flashing.

"Lo," I answered.

"Why 'ello there, Miss Marcus. You know, I really should have taken notice of your last name more because it's just like Talon's." Last week, shit had hit the fan in Zara's life. Her arsehole ex, who used to beat, belittle, and rape her, had discovered Zara's whereabouts. At least we believed he had since her parents had not long died and her brother found her because of it. We all suspected her brother, Mattie, could have been followed, leading David Goodwill right to her doorstep. I found the information out the day Zara didn't come into work, and I'd called. Only, instead of speaking with Zara, I got her annoying friend, and when she told me Zara wasn't coming in and to mind my own business, I knew something was up. I went to her house and found my brother in her living room. At first I was shocked to see him.

However, I should have realised it was only a matter of time before Talon had his sights set on Zara since she was always her stunning, goofy self. I'd learnt it'd taken him two years. Talon must have lost his touch with women. Then again, Zara had a past where it caused her to be standoffish with men.

By the end of it, Talon and I both agreed Zara would have protection, not only from his Hawks members but from me and my crew.

Smiling, I knew she was drunk from her slurring words. However, to mess with her, I asked, "Zara?"

"Yeah?"

"Are you drunk?"

"Maybe a wee little bit, and I thought, I'm having a few drinks with Deanna and Julian, and I was missing someone, and that someone was you. Now get your behind here and drink with us," she ordered.

My nose screwed up at hearing her friend's name Deanna. She and I had a hate-slash-hate relationship. I thought the woman a bitch, but Zara seemed to like her. At least I could give Deanna shit and she took it or gave it back. That was entertaining. "I doubt Barbie"—my name for Deanna since she looked like one—"wants me there."

"Oh, don't mind her. She's all full of shit bein' a hater."

"No, I'm not," I heard Deanna yell in the background.

Rolling my eyes, I told her, "I can't anyway. I'm still at work and I've got some filing to finish."

Of course, Zara being Zara, she got her way in the end. She decided a trip to work was what was needed. At least then I could keep an eye on her while she was here. I also knew she'd show with Hawks men at her back, and she did. Griz, Pick, and Blue wandered in after Zara, Deanna, and Julian, who was Zara's brother's boyfriend and a hoot to be around.

It didn't take long, after numerous drinks, for the conversation to shift to dirtier things.

The current was our first experience having sex. Julian had just told his tale and it was my turn. Only that wasn't the one I wanted to talk about.

"It wasn't until I met Travis that I was introduced to receiving it hard. God, I loved it when he used to pound into me, and let me tell you, he was huge. Delicious." I licked my lips at the thought of hot Travis back in university.

He was the one I would always miss. The one I could have married if our lives hadn't changed and our ambitions were different.

Regret always flew through my chest when I thought of Travis.

Only I knew, from searching, what his life was like nowadays, and I didn't want any part of it, or him.

That thought saddened me too. Why did he have to change so much?

I blinked and jolted when Griz clipped, "Enough." I glanced around, obviously missing something. "I don't wanna hear any more of this shit."

"Aw," Julian cooed.

Pick groaned. "No offense, man, but we had to hear about your first time. That was enough."

"You know what?" Zara said.

"What?" Julian, Deanna, and I asked at the same time, causing us all to laugh.

"I need music."

"Yeah." I nodded. "That'd be a grand idea. I want to dance." I smiled. A distraction from my thoughts would be awesome. Only my smile faded when I realised something. "But I haven't got anything here to listen to it on."

"Not even a radio?" Julian asked.

"Nope. But hey, there's a bar just down the road—"

"Fuck no," Blue said.

"Yes. Yes, I like that idea." Zara clapped, and once more, I was smiling, because again, Zara would get her way. It wasn't that she was spoilt per se, she was just loved by Talon and in return, the Hawks members would do anything for her. She added, "Come on, guys, it's just down the road, like five places away. We can walk. Nothing's gonna happen."

The crowded bar was dim and rowdy. We drank some more, danced, and had a great time. The only part I could have done without was Zara talking about my brother and wondering if he could be quiet during sex. I even banged my head against the back of the booth where the Hawks men sat.

Blue, Pick, and Griz quickly left. "Maybe I should join them. I really don't feel like hearing about what my brother gets up to in bed. It'll probably cause me to chuck." I actually did feel sick to the stomach.

"Block your ears," Deanna said.

For the sake of my sanity, I did just that. They kept talking while I glanced around the bar; that was how I caught some other bikers, who weren't Hawks, saunter up. They tried to cotton onto Zara. I was about to tell them where to go, but Griz came up and told them we were Hawks property. I wanted to scoff I wasn't anyone's property, but I didn't. I knew when to keep my mouth shut. I got out of the booth just as Blue ordered Zara to go dance.

Usually, I'd be all for kicking arse if needed, but I wanted to keep a better eye on Zara, so I went back out onto the dance floor with them.

Since nothing had happened all night, I thought I would be fine to go and get us some drinks. It was stupid of me to think that.

It was a foolish and dangerous mistake.

I also didn't think Zara would leave the group, yet she had. She must have because next, I saw her being carried over someone's shoulder outside. Not seeing Deanna, Julian, or any of the Hawks guys, I put the drinks down and hurried after them.

Outside, I took a lungful of air and scanned the streets. I spotted another guy with the one who was throwing Zara into the back of a car.

"Fuck," I barked. I didn't have my car, but I had to follow. When my eyes landed on a parked car, I knew I was about to do something I shouldn't.

Talon had taught me to jack cars at a young age. Thankfully those skills were still with me. Once I managed to get the car started, I booked it after the vehicle that held Zara before it disappeared out of sight. It was already way down the road.

Fear gripped my heart. It wasn't fear for myself, but for Zara.

She'd already been through enough in life. I didn't want anything to happen to her.

If I didn't know Talon loved her more than his own life, I would have stepped between them and made sure she knew who Talon had been. But since spending some time with both of them, I could see how taken they were with each other, and it wasn't my right to stop what was happening.

Christ, I had to warn the brothers at the bar. Pulling out my phone, I made a quick call. When Griz answered, I rushed out, "Zara's been taken. I'm in pursuit. I'll get her back to the bar. Don't leave."

"Fuck," he roared.

"I'll get her back," I promised.

"You'd better. I'll ring Talon—"

"No! Wait. Give me an hour. I can do this."

Silence greeted me on the other end for a moment and

then, "Fine," he clipped and hung up. Thank Christ I was at least smart enough to have my gun in the back of my jeans with my jacket covering it.

This was the type of shit I was born for. The thrill of the hunt. I would make these motherfuckers pay in one way or another. No one took from the Marcus family. No matter what type of business we were in.

I'd lost count of the time I'd been following at a distance. I started to slow when they pulled off into a driveway with an electric gate out front. There was a guard station at the side and security inside. One guy. Without making a scene, I sped up and drove by as if I wasn't following the dickheads' every move. The place was huge. Some jerkoff either had little dick syndrome or just liked to flaunt his riches.

Down the road, I pulled off to the side and thought of my options. I could just pull up to the gate and hope they'd open if I told them I was some hooker there to see whoever was behind the gate.

Shit, I suddenly felt like I was about to see the big and powerful Oz.

There was also the option of sneaking through the woods that surrounded the property. Surely the whole place wasn't guarded. Then again, the estate looked as if it'd have cameras everywhere.

Front door it was.

At least I'd stolen somewhat of a flashy car; it could help get me in.

Turning the car around, I drove to the gate and parked just outside it. The guy in the guard station stepped out with a glare.

"Who're you?"

"Hey, baby. I'm here to see the boss."

The guy eyed me. Yeah, I didn't exactly look like a slut in jeans and a tee, but the guy could be stupid.

"Move the fuck along. Boss doesn't want to be disturbed."

All right, he wasn't stupid. I needed to get in another way.

"Aw, but, baby, he'll wanna see me." I opened the door, hitting him in the gut. He gasped, hunched a little. "Shit, so sorry, baby. Let me rub it for you." Quickly, I moved out and around. As he was starting to stand, my fist met with the side of his face.

To my shock and elation, he fell to the ground, passed out cold.

"Seriously?" I asked his unconscious form with my hands on my hips. "You couldn't put up a fight?" I grumbled, rocking back and forth on my feet. "Idiot." I grabbed his arms and started to drag the fool towards the guard station. The fucker was heavy, but I wasn't a weakling. In my line of work, I needed to stay physically fit. Still, the oaf was a struggle. Once he was in, I found some handcuffs and clicked them on his wrist and then to his desk, which was bolted to the wall. I unplugged the phone, threw it outside and checked him over. He had a two-way, which I pocketed, and a mobile, which was another thing I threw out the door before pressing the button to open the gate. I climbed back into the car and drove towards the house.

It was dark. The only places illuminated were the house and the guard station at the gate. I didn't even have the car headlights on, hoping it wouldn't attract attention. The place was eerily quiet, and I wondered where all the guards were. Unfortunately, I ran into one just as I got out of the car.

"Hey, you," was shouted.

I stopped, waved, and waited for the guy to come closer. "Hi. The guy at the gate let me in. I have a meeting with the boss."

He opened his mouth to say something, and since his eyes were raking over my body, he didn't see my fist coming. He stumbled back, blinking at me. Yeah, not many expected a small, slim woman to have power behind her punch. Before he gained back his brains I scrambled, I ran at him and curled my arm around his neck. Swinging around his back, I used my other hand and gripped my arm, holding him tight in a choke-hold. He struggled, trying to buck me off, but I wrapped my legs around his waist and tightened my grip. He fell to his knees, tapping my arm. It wasn't until he passed out that I let go and stood, dusting myself off.

I quickly searched him, throwing his phone into the bushes near the house. I didn't have anything to tie him up with, and there was no time to look. I had to get to Zara in case anything was happening. Leaving him where he was, I hoped I got in and out before he woke.

Pulling out my gun, I stalked to the front door. Finding it unlocked, I sighed in relief and went straight in. The front hall was lit. Voices came down the hall; one was female. Hoping it was Zara, I headed in that direction.

I was almost to the end of the hall when a door opened right in front of me. The guy who'd carried Zara out of the bar strolled out but stopped when he spotted me. His eyes widened as he made a dive for me, which was stupid. I stepped back and hit him in the head with the end of my gun. He dropped to the floor.

I seriously had to wonder who the hell the boss was and why he would hire such idiots.

Stepping over him, I pushed through the door, gun raised, and froze.

"Travis?" Recognition swarmed me. Travis. *Travis Stewart.* Seeing him sitting behind the desk, foolish or not, I relaxed a little. My gaze shifted to Zara. She seemed okay as she sat opposite the desk staring over at me and then to Travis and back to me.

Of course she had to open her mouth and say, "That's your Travis?" She gasped and turned back to Travis with an inquisitive look.

"Violet. What are you doing here?" Travis asked, shock clear in his voice.

Shaking my head, I placed my gun in the back of my jeans. "I came for Zara." I made my way over to stand beside her.

"Where are my men?" Travis asked, his lips twitching.

I shrugged. "Unconscious. Travis, what's going on here? Why kidnap Zara?"

"Pam here told me Zara abused her in front of my child. I couldn't stand for that. I needed to have a word with her."

My chest burned at the knowledge of Travis having a child, but I pushed it down. I glanced to the woman standing beside Travis. I scoffed at the ridiculousness. "Zara wouldn't hurt a fly." I jerked my head Pam's way. "She's lying."

"I am not," the slut screeched.

"Oh, just give it up," Zara said. Then her attention went to Travis. "Ask my man. He'll tell you."

"Travis," I called. When his eyes came to me, I added, "you *really* should have gone about this in a different way."

A single brow rose. "Why?"

"She's Hawks property."

"Fuck," he bit out. "Whose?"

"Talon Marcus."

"Christ," he burst out with and turned on Pam. She took a few steps back, understandable because of the way Travis scowled at her. "Get the fuck out of my house. You lied, and now I have this shit to fix. You're fuckin' lucky I don't kill you. You stupid bitch, in front of my baby, you whored yourself?" Travis ran a frustrated hand through his salt and pepper hair.

A few years older than me, he'd definitely aged well. "Leave. Now."

I wanted to leave along with her. I didn't want to talk to him more or look at him. It brought up the memories I'd locked away.

He'd changed too much.

Only seeing him.... No, I'd ignore my body's reaction, and once out of this room, I'd forget about him again.

He wasn't worth it. He would never give up his business, and I was pretty sure I couldn't be with a man who was known as the biggest pimp in Victoria.

I would have to walk out and forget him again.

I had to.

Because if I was stubborn enough to lose my brother over how Talon had run his life, I wouldn't budge on my opinion of Travis's business and date him.

It'd also save a lot of hurt from the chance of losing him down the track.

# CHAPTER THREE

## VIOLET

*W*hen Pam ran from the room, Travis cursed up a storm and started pacing, only to stop behind his desk again. "I am truly sorry for this, Zara." His eyes slid to me. "When will I hear from Talon?"

"Not sure. He doesn't know yet."

Zara scoffed and asked, "How'd you pull that off?"

"I told the guys I'd be able to get you back before he found out." I didn't mention I begged for the trust and time to do it without Talon knowing. "It was just lucky I saw those idiots leaving with you over one's shoulder. I followed and rang Griz on the way. He freaked. I told him I'd have you back soon, so we better get going." Why I explained so much, I didn't know. It could've had something to do with the fact I could feel Travis's gaze on me.

"Wow, you're like a super-agent." Zara grinned.

"Yes." I glanced to Travis to see him smile appreciatively while his burning gaze ran over my body. I was grateful when he looked back to Zara. "Please let me know if there is anything I can do for you. Again, I am sorry for the way my men treated you, and for this… terrible misunderstanding. I'm sure I'll be hearing from Talon soon."

Zara's smile warmed. Fucking hell, she was starting to trust Travis, and that could lead to her liking him, wanting him in her circle of friends. That wasn't good when I'd be trying to get away from him. "Don't worry too much; it wasn't so bad, and I'll let Talon know that. I'm just thankful you know what a… nasty person your girlfriend is now."

Wait… that was his girlfriend? That big-breasted blonde slut? I clenched my jaw from laughing or yelling at him—I hadn't made up my mind.

Zara went on, oblivious to my brain overloading, "No one needs that around their child."

There it was again, a reminder Travis had a child. It was obvious Pam wasn't the mother, so who was?

Hang on, I didn't care.

I had to remember that.

"That's true." Travis nodded. "You sound like you speak from experience."

She did. Zara had her little girl, and she didn't want Maya around her ex, Maya's real father.

"I have a six-year-old daughter." She smiled proudly. "It was just lucky I got away from my nasty before it could touch her."

Jesus, they were bonding. I had to put a stop to it.

"Zara, we better go," I told her without looking at Travis.

"Maybe one day, when we have more time, you could explain further on that topic," Travis offered.

Zara cocked her head to the side; there she went accepting him. Fuck it.

She smiled and replied, "You know what, maybe one day I will. And I'm sure Violet would love to come along as well."

Like hell I would.

My eyes narrowed at Travis's smirk. "That would be wonderful. Coffee with two beautiful women."

Gag. He could shove his buttery words up his arse. I bit my tongue to keep my words at bay. I wouldn't cause a scene. I just had to make it out of there and forget him.

"Alrighty," Zara said, standing. "I'll be in touch. It was nice to meet you, Travis, and I'm glad it was you who kidnapped me."

I couldn't help but laugh at her words. She was crazy, in a fun way. Travis spewed more flowery words Zara's way before we left, words I blocked out as I stood at the door waiting for this puke fest to be over so I could get on with my life without seeing Travis again. In the end, I took her arm and pulled her from the room as the last goodbyes were had.

Zara gave me a look on the way out, probably wondering why I ignored Travis's goodbye. Only I didn't want to talk about it. About him.

Thankfully, she left it alone and focused on the car I'd stolen. "Whose is this?"

We both climbed in before I answered with, "Not sure. I had to find something quick to follow. But at least I'll be dropping it back, and hopefully, whoever this baby belongs to, they will be none the wiser."

We looked at each other and started laughing.

It was a wild night, and I was sure there would be more to come once Talon found out what had happened. Instead of wanting to see the show though, the idea of home, bath, book, and bed sounded like a nice, calming night compared to having to hear Talon rant and rave. And a good book would be a distraction from the man back at that obnoxious house.

## TRAVIS

Violet Marcus.

Of all the people to walk into my house with a gun raised, ready to kick some arse, it wouldn't have been Violet I'd imagined.

She looked amazing.

Sexy as fuck.

Though, she always had been.

God. Violet Marcus.

The woman I loved. The woman who still held a part of my heart. The woman I'd moved to town to chase. She was also the woman who looked at me like she wanted nothing to do with me.

I didn't like it.

I wouldn't accept it.

I knew one day I would have Violet back in my life. She never strayed from my mind. We were made for each other. She may not see it yet, obvious from her surprise and displeasure, but I hoped one day she would.

She'd always deserved better, she really did, but seeing her after so long had my resolve melting. Emotions rose and memories bombarded me. I'd promised her many years ago when we parted it wouldn't be forever. I was there to make good on my promise. Despite the years away from each other, I knew she was the only woman for me.

Could I have a chance at winning the private investigator, a woman who toed the line, over? My life, my past, my people, were dirty in the worst way.

Women sold their bodies for me. They had sex for me.

As the French would say, I was a souteneur, a protector of the women who worked for me. Others would just call me a pimp.

I was other things as well... but I had no idea if Violet would open her eyes and see what else, to see I was more.

Time would tell.

I had an in with Zara, and I would take it if it meant being in Violet's life one way or another.

It was after I'd fired and taught a lesson to my fucking pathetic hired help that I stood back in the library staring out the window, with my bourbon in hand, when my door burst open. I didn't turn, already expecting him.

"Talon," I called.

"Travis. You fuckin' wanna tell me what the fuck happened." He didn't ask; he never would. It was always a demand, much like the way I was with my people.

Turning, I leaned back against the window and took in Talon standing near the chair his lady had occupied not too many hours ago. A couple of his men were at his back. "I'm sure your sweet woman told you all about it."

"When you came to me, telling me your business won't touch my streets, I *let* you move to Ballarat. Move into *my* territory. Do *not* make me fuckin' regret it."

"You have my word no harm will come to you and yours from my hands or my people."

"Already fuckin' happened, Travis, and it doesn't sit well with me."

I sipped my drink and moved forward. "The men who touched your woman have been taken care of."

"They breathin'?"

"Barely."

"Good." He uncrossed his arms from his chest and gripped the back of the chair in front of him. "Know your history. Know who you were to my sister. Don't think, since seein' her tonight, that history will repeat itself."

"Now, Talon—"

"Don't fuck with me and mine, Travis. If you heed my warnin', then there won't be a problem."

I nodded once. Knowing it wasn't the time to fight for what I wanted with his sister yet, not until I won her over. Maybe even Zara, since she could put a good word in for me with her man. It could just save my life.

Talon said no more. Instead, he turned and moved out of the room with his men following. After pulling out my chair, I sat down and moved the mouse enough to bring my sleeping computer to life. The screen showed what I already wanted.

My daughter sleeping peacefully in her room two stories above me. I touched the screen, over her cheek. Izzy was such a sweet, innocent girl. Still so unaware of how life could tear you to pieces. I could only hope life for her, when she grew, would be gentle. She was like how I was when I was a child. Eyes closed to the world until my parents died in a train accident and my life changed into something cruel.

*I* made my life better because I didn't want anyone I loved to suffer like I had.

So I would try my best to make sure my daughter had a life where she didn't need to feel fear of anything. As long as she stayed away from her poisonous mother.

When my phone rang, I scowled down at it. It was after midnight. All my employees knew not to disturb me this late unless it was important, which was why I picked it up without glancing to the caller ID.

"Yeah?"

"Devin here. Just intercepted a call Violet Marcus got and thought you should know. Zara Alexander, her secretary, was kidnapped—"

"I know, that was—"

"No. Heard about that from Link, this just happened. A guy named Julian rang Violet on the way to the compound to inform Talon about what went down with Zara. Her ex, David Goodwill, got to her."

"Fuck." I stood, pulling out a gun from my drawer, holstering it under my jacket. "Keep me posted," I ordered and strode to the door, pocketing my phone. If they thought it was weird I was turning up in the middle of a crisis, I would come clean about how I knew. Until then, since Zara meant something to Violet, I would offer my assistance in any way.

I wouldn't be too far behind Talon. Link had arrived at the house to watch Izzy, just as I was getting to the front door.

The drive took me less time than I thought it would. As I pulled into the Hawks compound car park, it was just behind Violet. The man, Warden, got out of her car. She must have picked him up in case she needed more help before heading straight to her brother. Then I saw her glowering at me as she climbed out. I parked, got out, and strode her way.

"I heard what happened. I've come to offer my help."

She studied me for a moment, then nodded, and all three of us ran into the compound.

"What's going on?" Violet asked, stopping beside her brother.

"In short, I was betrayed by two of my brothers. Zara and the kids have been taken to David."

"Fuck," Warden whispered.

"Christ, no," Vi uttered.

"What can we do?" I asked. Talon's upper lip raised at me. He didn't want me there, but he would suck it up and do anything for his family. It would be what I would do.

When Talon didn't say anything, his expression dropped to nothing but the pain he was feeling inside, his second in command came forward and ordered, "Violet, you stay here with Deanna and man the phones. Travis, see if you can find out where David is situated right now through your sources.

Warden, you'll go with Blue. Once I call him into the hospital, you'll need to talk to Pick. Talon…."

Talon grinned. It wasn't a fucking nice one. "We're going to talk to Rocko."

I moved to the side and called Link. "Yeah?" he answered.

"Need everything on David Goodwill. Put all men onto it. He's in Victoria somewhere, and we have to find the fucker."

"On it," Link responded before hanging up.

I pocketed my phone and pulled Violet aside. She stared up at me, waiting. I didn't have a fucking clue what I wanted to say, but I'd overheard she, along with Deanna, argued to go with Talon instead of being left back. It could lead to dangerous situations.

"Violet—"

"Save it, I don't—"

I gripped her arms, pulled her close, and slammed my lips down onto hers. She froze, but I was determined. After a beat, and when I ran my tongue over her lips, she finally melted into me.

Just like she used to.

Even when pissed at me.

It was as if she couldn't resist my mouth, my taste.

Breaking the kiss, I ordered, "You'd better stay safe so we can talk and repeat that."

For a moment, her eyes warmed and she nodded. Then it was as if a switch was turned on and she shook her head. Eyes clearing, narrowing.

"You need to stay away from me, Travis, if you want to keep your balls intact."

Grinning, I watched as she stormed out of the room following Talon.

At least she was thinking about my balls.

It was a start.

Taking out my phone again, I walked from the compound and headed for my car. I had a few of my own calls to make. Someone had better come through for me, or they'd be out of my business in the future.

I wasn't the biggest pimp in Victoria for no reason. I had many clients owing me favours, and some of them were about to be called in.

# CHAPTER FOUR

## VIOLET

*F*uck Travis and his lips. The feel of them on me was seared into my brain. Why did the dickhead have to kiss me like he was worried about me? Hell, maybe he was, but he had no right to.

I sat at my computer fuming about it and the fact we were running out of leads to find Zara. Rocko, the Venom MC president, gave us addresses and number plates of the guys who were helping Vic, Talon's dead, betraying brothers. The ones who were delivering Zara to David. The other betraying brother, Pick, had redeemed himself in one way by saving Zara's brother and his partner from Vic's gun by getting shot himself. I knew he would pay by my brother's hands, though, and he'd deserve it.

I hated seeing Talon in pain. It gutted me to see my brother on the verge of losing it. Just from the way he fought to find them showed me the man he'd become—a good man, one who found the perfect woman for him. Anyone could see he loved Zara and the kids with his life. He couldn't and wouldn't live without them. I was proud, once again, to call him my brother.

We had to get them all back. For Talon, for the Hawks, and for even me.

I wanted more time with my nephew, Cody, Talon's son, who I hardly knew. I wanted to see Zara giving Talon a hard time. I just wanted more time with everyone I loved.

"Anything?" Talon asked, desperation in his tone.

"Talon, I'm not that frigging fast, give me a minute," I answered. "I'll send Chuck to their houses, but I doubt they're there. They would have taken them to David straight away so they could be paid," I explained and then picked up my phone.

I kept Chuck on the line while he drove to the houses. "Nothing, Vi," he said with a sigh. "They ain't at either house."

"Shit," I whispered.

Talon, with the phone to his ear, called out, "Violet, how we doing?"

"Zip. I've got Chuck on the line. There's no one at their houses. Their cars are in their frigging drives. I've got nothing else to go on." Panic showed in my voice. "I'm sorry."

"Jesus Christ," Talon whispered. Torment flashed in and out of his eyes. He said into the phone, "No. Fuck, brother. We have to find them—" I stood as Talon tensed, listening. "Blue?" he snarled. "Brother," he demanded. His shoulders sagged, his eyes closed, I got close. "Text me the address. I'll meet you there." He hung up and told us, "Travis got a location. Let's go."

Travis had come through.

That was… nice. But, nope, I wouldn't think about that.

"Talon, wait," I called when a thought crossed my mind.

"What, woman? I gotta get my family."

"You and Griz need my guns. If the bullets are traced, I'm covered for being a PI. You're not."

My brother closed his eyes. He knew I was protecting him. He felt it deep, but he had to know when it came to matters of family, I would always have his back. Ignoring Deanna and Griz, I opened my gun safe under my desk, got out three, and walked over to Talon. Handing one to Griz, then to Talon, I slipped the other into the back of my jeans.

Talon caught my gaze. "There could be a lotta people goin' down today, Vi. You ready for this?"

"Fuck yeah." I smiled. We'd get Zara and the kids back. Talon would continue living a happy life with a woman he *did* deserve, and I would gain back my brother and his family.

"Let's move then." Talon grinned back at me.

We met the other Hawks members. Once we were out of the car, Blue asked, "What's the plan?"

Talon sucked in a breath. "We need to be fast, get in and get out. The warehouse is a block away at the end of a dead-end street. Not much goes on in these parts, so there shouldn't be any witnesses we'd need to buy off." Talon stopped; fury crossed his features, and I was sure I still knew my brother enough to know he'd be thinking he was wasting his time explaining when all he wanted to do was get in there and out with his family.

Stepping up, I rested my hand on his arm. He glanced down at me. "We go in on foot from here. We don't want them knowing we're coming." I glanced over Blue's shoulder to see Warden pull in. I smiled. "Good, just in time." Warden climbed out and went to the back of the car, opening the trunk. I'd asked him to make a stop for me. "Everyone needs to swap out their weapons for one of ours," I shouted to the brothers.

"Shit, Vi," Talon groaned, emotions rode his voice. "How the fuck are you going to explain firing off twenty or so guns to the cops?"

I shrugged. "We'll deal with that when the time comes." He shook his head. I shifted closer. "Do you think Zara would want her man in jail after just saving her?" I asked. She wouldn't, and I wouldn't want to actually see my brother in jail after he'd cleaned his life and the lives of his members up. This was different. It was for family, and the only people who would be harmed were ones who shouldn't exist anyway. "No. Do it for her, Talon." He eyed me, searching for something. He must have found it because he nodded.

Tears welled, but I blinked them away, and thankfully, Barbie, Zara's best friend and my arch nemesis, piped up with, "Do I get a fuckin' gun now?"

"No," Griz answered with a growl to his tone. "You stick with me, princess."

Even though the woman annoyed the fuck out of me, she had balls; I would give her that. I'd also *try* to get along with her for Zara. If only she didn't piss me off.

When Talon called, "Right, let's roll out," I stopped them once more. He groaned. "What?"

"Send Warden in there first, he'll get any cameras there are offline."

Talon looked to my employee with doubt in his eyes. Yes, Warden was on the tall and huge side, but he was stealthy. No one detected him before he wanted them to know he was there. Talon nodded, then paced as we waited. Warden came back, tipped his chin and said, "Coast's clear." Talon spread his brothers out around the warehouse. I stayed at his side, along with Griz and Deanna.

We made our way to the front door, surprisingly not running into anyone. Reminded me of Travis's house. A moment later, Blue ran around the corner and informed us his team had taken out five men. Talon replied with a chin lift and walked up to the front door. It was locked. Talon stepped back, no doubt ready to kick it in, when Deanna moved up and knocked on the door. We all stared at her.

Seconds later, the front door opened. A guy in a biker vest with a Vicious club patch stood in it. He went to grab a two-way until Deanna punched him in the face. It was times like that I could actually like the woman.

We left Blue to deal with him and walked into the house. Silently, we took the stairs when we heard a gunshot sound in the distance. My heart cracked to allow the panic through.

"Shit, shit," Deanna chanted.

We stopped at the end of a hallway. Talon signalled us to stay quiet as he moved to the first door. It revealed nothing. Griz, at the second, showed one of Rocko's, the Vicious president, men. Griz took care of him with one hit. I went to the next door. Nothing.

This shit started to piss me off. Though, it was better than letting the fear take control. Talon tried the fourth door. It was locked, so I stepped up, took out my lock picking kit, and kneeled on the floor. Within seconds, it clicked open. I moved out of the way, so Talon could open the door; he stepped in with his gun raised.

Noises touched my ears, leading my eyes to the corner of the room where I saw four bodies huddled together. Talon saw it as well. Then we heard, "Dad?"

Cody. Dear God, it was Cody.

"Told ya he'd come," Cody said to the other people.

"Talon," Maya, Zara's little girl, cried as she ran at my brother. He locked his body as she hit against him. He swung her up and hugged her close, gesturing to Cody to come to him.

"Richard? Nancy?" Deanna asked.

The older couple stood. The man stepped forward more into the light from the hallway. "Why, hey there, Deanna girl."

"Oh my God." Deanna gasped.

Richard? Nancy? My brain clicked where I'd heard those names. Zara's parents. They were alive.

"My, my, it's so good to see you, Deanna, and in the flesh instead of Skype," Nancy said, stepping around Richard. She looked just like her daughter, only older. My chest expanded, filling with joy for Zara. Nancy went on, causing Deanna and me to laugh, "And you're just a hot piece of eye candy."

Turning towards the door, I raised my gun, but the foot-steps I heard were only Griz's. In his arms, he carried a teen girl. "Found her in a room. She's unconscious but alive." He lay her on a bed.

"Have you seen Zara?" Talon asked her parents.

"Oh my. No wonder my girl couldn't resist you with a voice like that," Nancy commented. Talon's mouth dropped a little before he snapped it shut; I could tell he wanted to yell but refrained.

"Nance, focus. We saw her earlier, but that was a few hours ago. We don't know where she is," Richard told him.

Another gunshot sounded, and it wasn't far from where we were.

"Fuck," Talon clipped. He put Maya on her feet. "Stay here with your grandparents. Deanna, you gotta stay here with the girl in case she's gonna be trouble." It was a smart move, giving her something to do so she wouldn't rant and rave about being left behind.

"Sure, boss," she replied, taking out a taser.

Talon spoke to Richard, Maya, and Cody before we left the room, just as another gunshot sounded. We bolted for the door at the end. Talon kicked it in and entered. I was hot on his tail, only to freeze for a second.

Blood.

So much blood surrounded Zara on the couch.

"Who the hell are you?" David asked.

Ignoring him, knowing my brother and Griz had him, I went for Zara. Kneeling beside her, I didn't know if I should touch her. Still, I pressed my fingers against her neck.

"Tell me she's breathing," Talon demanded.

Zara's eyes fluttered. "H-honey?" She started coughing. I ran my hands over her, my jaw clenching tighter and tighter. My stomach dipped in dread.

"Christ, Talon. We have to get her outta here. She's got three gunshot wounds and she's been beaten."

"You're not taking her," David yelled.

"Back the fuck up," Talon roared. "You bloodied my woman, you beat her, raped her, and fuckin' shot her. Fuck!" A shot fired behind me. Right away I knew it wasn't Talon getting shot because he wouldn't cry out like a piece of weak shit.

"Zara, it's going to be okay. We've got you," I whispered, gently lifting her hair from her face. She nodded, only to wince.

"Damn it," David screamed.

"Talon!" I yelled. "We have to go, and now."

"Griz, take him. Clean this. I'm getting my woman outta here."

"Sure, brother," Griz replied.

Talon stopped beside the couch, kneeling. He swallowed over and over at the sight of his woman. It was bad, very bad. I wanted to cry, scream, kick something, but I didn't. I'd hold it back.

"Jesus, babe," Talon whispered.

"I-I k-knew you'd come. Kids? Parents?"

He ran a hand down her cheek softly. "They're safe. Now let's get you safe." We both knew there wouldn't be time to wait for paramedics. Talon picked her up as gently as he could, but she still cried out. My jaw clenched, along with my fists.

"Vi, clear the way. Make sure the kids don't see."

"On it," I said, running from the room.

We made it out without a problem. I raced to the car Warden just exited and got in the driver seat. "She okay?" Warden asked through the passenger-side window.

I shook my head. "Get the back door open. Help Talon get her in."

He nodded and straightened just as Talon came out of the house with Zara in his arms. My breath hiccupped. I beat down my emotions once more.

"Talon?"

"She's passed out," he told me, his face hard. They managed to get her into the car and on Talon's lap. Warden jumped in the front, and I drove off like hellhounds were chasing us, knowing Talon would brace for my erratic driving. Even Warden leaned through to the back and helped hold her still. He would surely be bruised tomorrow for it.

"Nearly there, kitten. Hold on for me," he begged, kissing her forehead. "Fuck," he snarled low.

I bit my bottom lip to keep from crying. Hated seeing Zara on the edge of.... I couldn't bring myself to think it, say it. What I also hated with my whole being, was seeing my brother crushed with anguish.

The tyres screeched when I pulled up at the back of the hospital, the emergency area. Sniffing, I got out as people stormed out. "You can't park—"

I waved my arms, they paused. "Help." I pointed to the back

of the car. "She needs help. Three gunshot wounds and she's been beaten."

They rushed forward, one calling for a trolley. From there on, it was go, go, go. Talon nearly went berserk when they wouldn't let him through with her. I grabbed his arms and whispered into his ear, "They need to do their work. Let her go so they can work, Talon. Please."

He stilled, then nodded. The emergency team raced through the halls while we were led into the waiting room.

I sat beside Talon with my arm around his shoulders, and we waited. Brothers arrived. Griz deflected the cops, informing them what went on at the warehouse. Though, it wasn't the full truth of course. Deanna kicked up a stink about not getting her hands on David, until Talon informed her there was still time. Her smile was evil. Nancy, Richard, and the kids arrived freshly showered, and they all surrounded Talon. It wasn't until a police officer said some words Talon didn't want to hear, by saying they would need Zara's statement *if* she pulled through, that my brother lost it once more and he hit the man.

The brothers crowded Talon. I pulled the cop aside while he ranted about pressing charges, and told him, "You know who he is. He lives hard. Do you think he doesn't love just as hard? The woman in there is his world, and you saying *if* she pulled through doesn't cut it for him. Give the guy a break. Please."

The cop sucked in a breath, glanced at Talon and then back to me. "I won't press charges."

I sighed. "We would appreciate it."

The room fell silent. I wasn't sure how long we waited until the doctor came through the doors. Her steps faltered a little on seeing Talon and his men. "Uh... family of Zara Edgingway?"

Talon stood, holding the kids close to him. "That's us."

"Oh, okay. I just wanted to say she's through surgery, and it looks like she's going to be okay."

I watched as Talon sank to his knees in relief, the kids going down with him, both crying. I closed my eyes, tipped my head back and mouthed, "Thank you."

# CHAPTER FIVE

## TRAVIS

She was likely to kill me for being here, but I knew she'd had a rough day. The good news had reached me that Zara and the kids were alive. But I still wanted to make sure Violet was okay.

I stood outside her door and knocked.

There were no footsteps, no sounds on the inside, so I looked behind me and caught sight of her car. She had to be home.

I knocked again.

"Go away, Travis," I heard from just behind the door.

"Violet, let me in."

"No. Go away."

"Violet, please. I've heard Zara and the kids are okay. I just had to check on you."

I heard a noise; it sounded like a sob. "Go. Away."

Reaching out, I touched her door. "Open the door, Lettie," I said, using the nickname I had given her back in university.

The door abruptly opened. Her eyes were filled with tears,

her cheeks stained from previous ones and her running make-up. Her hair a mess, but to me, she was still beautiful.

"Don't you dare call me that," she snapped, then wiped her nose using the back of her hand. "Leave me alone, Travis. If you think that kiss meant something, you're wrong. It was nothing. Just a moment and that moment ended when I walked away." She sniffed. "Go away." Violet went to slam the door in my face. I pushed it back and grabbed her wrist, hauling her into my arms.

"Don't," she cried.

"Zara will heal," I told her.

"I know," she yelled, pushing at my chest. She was tired, weakened in her state, or else I would have been on my arse.

"You're fine. Talon is, the kids are. Everything worked out," I told her, holding her tightly to me. Gradually, her struggling stopped and she slumped into me, her forehead hitting my chest.

"He shot her."

"I know."

"He beat her."

"I know," I whispered.

"How can someone be so cruel?" she asked, her voice cracking at the end. "In my line of work, I've seen some pigs, some mean bastards… but nothing like that."

"He will pay."

"He will, but Zara, the kids, they'll need time to heal, time to get past what he did to them."

"And they will. They'll have all the support in the world. Your brother will make sure of it."

She nodded against me, then stiffened. Pulling away, she glared up at me. I fought my smile. *There's my woman.* Rather than sharing my thoughts, I asked, "Can I come in for a coffee?"

"No," she bit out. Her body swayed, and she cursed under her breath. "However, I am going to use you. So you can come in and sit in the living room while I go to my room and sleep. Knowing someone else is in the house will help me. Can I use you, Travis?"

My lips twitched, causing her eyes to narrow even more.

"Yes." I nodded.

"This'll mean nothing," she warned.

"Just dinner."

Her head jerked back. "What? No way."

"Violet, dinner."

"No."

Funny she hadn't tried to close the door again. "Dinner," I demanded. She could use me all she liked, but I would be sure to get something in return. "Just a couple of hours with me while we eat. That's all I'm asking."

She groaned, running a hand over her face, and said, "Fine. I'm too tired to argue." With that, she turned and walked down the hall. I stepped in. Grinning, I locked the door and followed her.

When I entered the living room, I saw her walking to another doorway. There she turned. She looked from my feet up to my face, nodded, entered the room, and slammed the door behind her.

I got the message loud and clear. I wasn't to enter the room, and knowing her, if I tried, she would have a gun pointed at my face in seconds. Even if she did look exhausted.

Moving to the couch, I sat down, turned the TV on low, and leaned back. Pulling my phone free, I sent a text to Link.

**Staying. Get me a reservation at the club in Melbourne.**

**Link: She agreed to dinner?**

**Me: Reluctantly and I may have pushed for it.**

**Link: You're a dick.**

Me: Not something I don't know. How's business?

Link: Good. Be better if I was out there instead of babysitting.

Me: You know I only trust you with Izzy.

Link:

Me: Was that a fucking smiley face?

Link: Shit, was supposed to send that to Trisha.

Me: Sure.

Link: Fuck off. Stop annoying me so I can watch Shrek for the millionth time.

Me: I'm laughing.

Link: Why are you so fucking needy today?

Me: Suck me.

Link: Not even if you're dying. Now get lost. I've made the reservation. Have fun. Don't screw this up because I'm sick of hearing about how she's your one that got away. Your dream woman. Your... you get the damn point.

Me: I do. Have fun with Izzy.

Link: She wants to do my hair.

Me: I'm laughing again.

Link: Fuck off.

Laying my phone on the coffee table, I stood and made my way into the kitchen. Being in Violet's house felt strange, and yet, not. While I'd never been there before, the house smelled of Violet. Her scent had stayed locked in my mind since university. It brought up the memory of first seeing Violet in the cafeteria ready to kick some guy's arse because he brushed up against her the wrong way.

Even back then she'd been feisty. It wouldn't be until we'd started dating that I realised how sweet she could be behind closed doors.

I'd missed her.

I was wrong to leave her. I should have begged her to come with me.

Regret over leaving, even though we'd parted ways amicably, would always live inside of me because I had been the one to leave. In time, with her around me, I hoped that regret would heal.

Then again, when she found out what my line of work was, it was likely she'd run in the opposite direction.

Unless she already knew.

If she did, I would have thought she'd be up in my face about it by now. Admittedly, we hadn't had much time together, which would change. That was if she did accept me as I was, with my business and all.

It worried me she wouldn't. Then what would I do?

Fuck. I couldn't class what I felt as worry.

It was fear, deep in my gut, and it slowly burrowed into my chest.

Violet was above the law.

I was below.

Could our connection, once she accepted me in her life again, be enough for her?

Fucking hell, I had no clue, and not knowing was the worst.

I poured the coffee into the mug I found, which read, "Have I had my coffee? Then do not talk to me." It was Violet all over. She hated talking until she'd had at least two cups of coffee. Then it was as if her brain had woken and was ready for the day.

Smiling, I sipped my black coffee and glanced around the place. Nothing matched and yet it looked good. I saw the newspaper sitting on her bench. Picking it up, I leaned into the counter and flicked through the pages.

Nothing new, but it would keep me busy for a while and

hopefully keep me from going through Violet's things like I wanted to.

I knew I'd have to come clean about having her phones tapped.

She'd call me a stalker, a pervert, which I was both... but I did it when I first moved back because I wanted reassurance she wasn't connected to anyone she shouldn't have been, that she was safe within her work and the clients she took on. I hadn't been ready to face her. I needed all the information first to have in my back pocket to make sure I had a good fight before she shut the door in my face. There was also the fact I had to get rid of Pam.

I had to make sure Violet stayed safe while I did my dirty work. I didn't like she was a private investigator. Like she'd said, in her line of business, she'd met some bastards, and it concerned me to a point I had to make sure she didn't bite off more than she could chew.

Tapping her private phone was another excuse. It was so I could learn about her private life. What I learnt was that other than her employees, she didn't really have anyone she spoke with. She deserved more in life.

She deserved—

With my mug halfway to my mouth, I froze when a door slammed open. Quickly, I put my coffee down, pulled out my gun, and hid just behind the kitchen doorway.

Violet stomped in. She looked ready to take on anything and anyone.

"You," she snarled at me.

"Me?" I asked, putting my gun away, which she eyed. "I don't think an hour of sleep was enough for you, Violet."

"Don't get all smart on me, dickhead. You have some explaining to do."

I walked back to my coffee. Her eyes darkened when I lifted

the cup to my lips and sipped. There was zero sexual intensity in her gaze though; instead, it seemed murder was her only intent. "Explaining? About what?"

When her gaze shifted to her knife block and back, I knew it would be bad if she was already thinking of harming me.

"You tapped my phones," she fumed through clenched teeth.

Well, fuck.

Had my thinking been aloud?

"Warden called me. He thought it was time to check the system for any bugs. Guess what he found?"

"Bugs," I said calmly before sipping my drink.

She gripped the counter between us. "Fucking bugs, Travis. He traced the source. He found the company. He fucking found the goddamn motherfucking owner of that company. Guess who the owner is?"

My lips twitched, which wasn't good since she eyed the knife block again. "Me?"

"Yes," she hissed. "You. Tell me why you tapped my work and home phone, Travis? And it'd better be a good reason, or I'm thinking you would look good bathed in your own blood."

"Violet—"

"Explain," she yelled.

"If you just calm down—Fuck," I cursed when a vase came flying at my head.

"Do. Not. Tell. Me. To calm down."

That was certainly something to take note of.

"All right. You may not understand the reason for it right now, but one day you could."

She waved her hand around. "Keep talking."

I put my coffee down. "I've wanted to reach out to you since I moved back to Ballarat. I wasn't sure you would want me to. So instead, I reached out in a different way so I could assure myself you were protected."

"I have my men, Travis. You know this."

"I do." I ran a hand through my hair. "You've always been on my mind, Violet. Me tapping your phones was a mistake, but I don't regret it, or I wouldn't have been able to help with the Zara situation."

Her jaw clenched. "You're just fucking lucky you have that as an excuse. Ring your people, Travis. What you did was creepy as fuck. I've been on your mind, so you go behind my back and invade my life in a way I didn't know about." She shook her head. "Only stalkers do shit like that."

There was that word. Stalker.

Hell, I probably was one, but my worry for her overtook my mind more. "It will stop."

"Good. Now go."

"What?"

"Do you seriously think I would want anything to do with you knowing this? I've been on your mind? Man the hell up and come at me instead of doing scary shit like this. Did you honestly think I wouldn't find out?"

"I was going to tell you."

"Yeah? When?"

"After you've warmed to me being in your life."

"It's not happening, Travis. I don't want you to be in my life, and I don't want to be in yours either. Especially not with the way you have it. Prostitutes, Travis? Really?"

Christ, she did know. Of course she knew. I was dumb to think differently. Dumb to hope.

"Now, Violet, it's just a business."

She sighed, shaking her head. "I'm too tired for this shit. Just leave, Travis."

I started around the bench, and she backed up. "Violet,

46

please try to understand my actions for tapping your phones were made with good intentions. To have your back when someone else couldn't. I just wanted to protect you."

She glanced to the side. "I know. But it's still..." She shivered. "Wrong."

"I know. It was stupid of me. And my business—"

"Don't. We'll talk another day."

"Violet—" I snapped my mouth shut when my phone started ringing. It was Link's tone. He wouldn't ring unless something was wrong. Dread filled my gut. I ran into the living room and snatched up my phone. "Link?"

"That fuckin' pathetic bitch of an ex of yours is here wanting to see Izzy."

"Fuck," I clipped. "I'm on my way." I ended the call and made my way to the front door.

"What's wrong?" Violet called.

"Nothing."

"Travis, you can't just walk out of here looking ready to kill someone after a phone call and not tell me."

"Violet, it's not for you to worry about." I opened the door.

It wasn't, nothing in my life was for her to concern herself over... yet.

There wasn't a chance in hell I would subject Violet to Izzy's mother.

"Travis Stewart," she snapped, stomping my way. Her hand landed on the door, pushing it closed. "You owe me after what you've done. Tell me what's going on."

Straightening, I turned to her. She was right, I did owe her, but it wouldn't be— "What was that for?" I asked, rubbing my gut where she hit.

"You're thinking of not telling me. I might be able to help."

"You can't help. I have to go." I went for the door again. She slipped between me and it, crossing her arms over her chest. "Violet," I growled out.

"Travis."

"Fuck. It's my ex. She's at the house wanting to see Izzy, but I refuse to let her."

She nodded. "Right. Let me get changed."

"I don't have time to wait."

"That's all right. I'll meet you there." She raced off towards her room.

"Violet," I called. She turned at her doorway. "I don't want you around the evil bitch."

She laughed. "See you there."

"Violet—"

"You need to go. So go."

Frustrating woman. Still, I did have to go. Shit, this wasn't going to be good.

# CHAPTER SIX

## VIOLET

*S*ince my phone was in my hand, I made a quick call, putting it on speaker while I changed. "Vi," Warden said into the line. "Did you kill him?"

Laughing, I shook my head. "Not yet. Listen, I want you to do a search. Travis was married. I want you to find out everything you can on his ex."

"On it," he answered, and then hung up.

Dressed in jeans and a dark-blue blouse, I washed my face, tied my hair up, and slipped on my boots before rushing out of the house.

Wait... I paused on the front steps. Why was I rushing off to help Travis?

He'd tapped my phones.

My fucking phones.

Who did that to people? I didn't know what to think. I hated it, yet a small part of me understood it. In his weird way, he was doing it to protect me. But I swore to all the Gods out there, if he thought of doing something stupid like that again, I would rip his balls off and shove them up his arse.

Where had the promise to myself gone to stay away from him? Yet, there I was walking swiftly—I wouldn't call it running, just walking fast—to my car.

The fool confused me, muddled me, and it pissed me off.

One day. One goddamn day he was back in my life, and he was already in my head.

Yes, I'd known he was in Ballarat, but I never wanted to see him. Not since we were polar opposites in what we did in our jobs.

I slammed my hand onto the steering wheel as I drove down the road. Stupid man.

Why did he have to say I'd always been on his mind? How could I have been when he'd been married, had girlfriends? If that were the case, wouldn't he have come back to Ballarat a long time ago?

My phone rang when I was close to Travis's place. I pressed the button. "Warden."

"Her name's Kathleen Jaida. She's twenty-seven, been in rehab for the third time around. Drug addict." He paused. "Vi, Travis has a restraining order against her. She stabbed him when he was trying to protect their daughter. She was high at the time, and according to the report, she thought her daughter was the devil."

My stomach churned, and I rubbed at my aching chest.

She tried to kill her daughter. Stabbed Travis. All because of drugs.

"Got it."

"She gonna be a problem?"

"I don't think so. I can take her in for going against her restraining order."

"You're going to her?"

"She's at Travis's trying to get in to see the daughter. I'm heading there now to see if I can help."

"Want backup?"

"No. You know I got this."

Warden chuckled. "Yeah, I do. Then, want backup for Travis?"

"What do you mean?" I demanded.

He laughed again. "Woman, he wants you."

"He's not getting me."

"You got a past with him?"

"Yes. University days, but it doesn't matter. He tapped my phones. He's a pimp. He's not for me any longer."

Warden hummed under his breath.

"What?" I snapped.

"Nothin', Vi. Good luck, and call if you need help."

"I will. Later," I said, then hung up as I pulled into Travis's property. The gate was still open, so I drove through and saw Travis standing in his doorway. Another man, who was covered in tattoos—arms, neck, and no doubt body—stood outside the door and to the left of it. A woman, Kathleen I assumed, was up in Travis's face, yelling, waving her arms around erratically.

Parking, I climbed out. Everyone paused to take me in as I made my way up to the front door.

"Who the fuck is this?" Kathleen screeched.

Stopping beside them with my hands on my hips, I looked up to the tall bitch and said, "Violet Marcus. Private investigator. It's my understanding you're in breach of a restraining order. If you'll come with me calmly, I'll take you to the station."

I knew asking for calm wasn't the best move since I hated it when people told me to be calm. Kathleen was the same. She came at me and pushed me back. "I'm not going anywhere until I see my daughter, bitch."

"Ma'am—"

"Don't fucking call me ma'am." She went to push me again. I sidestepped her, and she stumbled forward, whirling to face me again.

"Fine. Kathleen, you can either leave right now and never return to this property, or I will take you in. I have the right to do so."

"Fuck you," she spat.

Sighing, I watched as she moved around me and got close to Travis. "Let me in to see Izzy, Travis."

"For the final time, Kathleen, no," he stated.

It was as if a switch flicked inside of her. She stepped closer, her expression softening, her body relaxing. Then her hand came out, and she managed to rub it down Travis's body, heading towards his junk when I leaped forward, gripped her hand hard enough she yelped, and pulled her away from him.

"Do. Not. Touch. Him." Realizing what I said, I quickly added, "Violation again against a restraining order." I twisted her arm behind her back and glanced to Travis. "What do you want to happen?"

I felt like slapping that smirk off his face. He was probably pleased I stopped her groping him. I only did it because she was sick and twisted. She had no clue what her actions and words could do to a little girl who could be listening inside.

Travis's face hardened when he looked to his ex. "Will you leave and never return?"

She didn't say anything, so I pulled her arm back tighter. She cried out. "I'll go."

Turning her, I released her arm and pushed her forward. Crossing my arms over my chest, I raised my brows when she turned back. I waited. When she didn't say anything, only glared, I gave her my back and faced Travis and the other silent man who stood with a huge grin on his face.

I listened to her footsteps, heard a car door open and then

slam. It wasn't until the car started and peeled out of the driveway that I said, "She's going to be trouble again."

Travis nodded. "I know."

"Ring the police, tell them about this incident. I'm sure you have cameras, so show them the footage. You want this on record...." I paused. "Unless you don't want her to go to jail."

The other man snorted.

Travis's upper lip raised. "I want her to rot."

I nodded. "Okay then. Get this on record, and if she comes back again, call the police. They'll arrest her."

"I will."

We stared at each other for a moment, but then a throat cleared.

Travis's eyes narrowed on his friend. "Link, this is Violet. Violet, Link."

Link's hand came my way. I took it and shook. He grinned. "Nice to meet you finally, Violet."

"Ah, yeah." I nodded, glancing down to my hand when Link didn't let go and kept shaking it.

"Good to see Travis has a good woman who's not shy to take care of situations."

My head whipped to Travis. He was already stepping up. His hand went over ours and I felt the pressure. "Want to drop her hand, Link?"

He chuckled. "Sure."

"What do you mean, woman?" I asked. "I'm not his woman. Did he tell you I was his woman?"

Link's eyes widened. "Ah." He coughed.

My gaze went to Travis. "Did you say I was your woman? One kiss, Travis, and I was in a panicked state. I told you nothing was going to happen between us."

"Violet." He smiled.

"Why are you smiling?" My jaw clenched.

"You came to help me. You stopped her from touching me."

"So?" I screeched. God, I sounded like his ex. Breathing deeply, I pinched the bridge of my nose and nodded to myself. "I am going to end up killing you."

Link laughed loudly. "Shit, I fuckin' love her myself."

"Link," Travis barked low and grumbly.

"Daddy?"

"Izzy, honey, no," a female called from inside.

I froze.

A little girl around five came running out the door and jumped. Travis turned in time to catch her. His face buried into her neck where he blew some raspberries.

Oh shit.

Fuck him. I would not defrost over the sight of him being sweet, cute, and yet all goddamn sexy at the same time.

He tapped my phones for God's sake.

A woman stepped out, puffing, her hand on her chest. "Sorry, she got away from me."

"That's because she's a monster." Travis grinned.

"I am not, Daddy. I'm a princess."

"Hmm, I'll have to see about that. You know, princesses eat all their vegetables. Will you eat yours tonight?"

Cuteness overload. I had to get out of here.

Stepping back, hoping no one would notice me, I got one foot on the steps behind me when the woman looked at me. She smiled. I didn't return it. I didn't know who she was.

"I'll try, Daddy," Izzy replied, causing Travis to laugh. Then he reached out, hooked his arm around the woman and tugged her into his side, kissing her temple.

I clenched my fists and jaw. I took another step back, glaring at them. With a quick glance to Link, I saw him not watching the couple, but me. He winked at me before he shot his hand out to the woman. "Trisha, come meet Violet." *She's not Travis's woman?* "Violet. This is my married sister, Trisha."

I scoffed, rolled my eyes, glared at Link, and scoffed again. "Not sure why you're adding married in there." I nodded to Trisha. "Nice to meet you, but I have to get going." I spun away.

"Violet," I heard, in a sweet, giggly voice. "Your name's pretty."

Fuck me. Could I ignore the child? Would it be rude?

Yes. Yes, it would be.

Holding my sigh in, I turned back around and smiled. "Thank you. So is Izzy." I waved. "Bye."

"You should stay for dinner," she added quickly.

Where was a gag when I needed one? Wait, it was wrong to gag kids, right? I was sure people would understand in this situation, one where I was trying to get away from her father, so I didn't melt and cave because he had tapped my phones.

He was also a pimp.

He pimped women out for sex so he could get money.

Slowly turning, I caught sight of Trisha and Link smiling, while Travis was at least grinning down at the floor.

"Thank you for the offer, but I didn't get much sleep last night, so I won't be good company." I waved again and managed another step.

"You can come another night. You have really pretty black hair. I wanna do your hair. Promise to wash my hands after dinner."

"Ah...." Shit, I had nothing. Her eyes were drawing me in.

"You can't say no to that cuteness," Link said. I shot a glare his way. He and Trisha laughed. I glanced back to Izzy. Dear Jesus, she was batting her lashes.

"Um, maybe one day... sure."

"Yay!" she screamed. "Tomorrow?"

"No, I have to—"

"The next day."

"Ah, probably not."

"The next?"

"We'll see."

"Yay! Daddy will ring you. Daddy, do you have Miss Violet's number?"

This kid was switched on for her age... or maybe I just didn't hang around children enough to know how smart and cunning they really were—something I would change soon, since I wanted to get to know my nephew, Cody, and even Zara's girl, Maya.

I really felt like I was being played.

"I do. I'll ring her, princess."

She smooshed his cheeks together in her tiny hands and yelled once more, "Yay!"

It was adorable.... No, it wasn't. "I've got to go. Nice meeting you, talk soon. Bye." Before Izzy could suggest anything else, like a sleepover, I made a mad dash for my car, got in, waved lamely, and drove off.

I was certain I'd just been outplayed by a little girl.

# CHAPTER SEVEN

## VIOLET

*A* week passed by the time my luck ran out. All right, I'd just run out of good excuses to decline my dinner invitation from Izzy, who was five. Travis had told me as such over the phone. Speaking of the phone, Travis had called me every damn day. Sometimes it wasn't even to ask about dinner, just to see what I was up to.

He'd ask about my day.

I could have, and probably should have, not answered his calls, but I begrudgingly admitted to myself that I wanted to hear from him. I'd always liked hearing his voice over the phone.

I was a glutton for punishment.

A punishment that could lead to me being hurt. Yes, I didn't like the fact he made money off women who sold their bodies for sex. The thought made me sick to the stomach. But I also knew it was an excuse to hide behind because it scared me how being around Travis was addictive.

He was the man I loved.

The only man I loved.

We parted, and I knew I wouldn't love another man like him.

I dated safe men. Men who weren't anything like Travis—strong-willed, smoking hot, and arrogant, yet sweet, and also protective.

Fear had me building my walls higher around Travis because I worried we would get close and then something else could come between us. I wasn't sure watching him walk away a second time would be good on me, regardless of the first time we'd both agreed to separate. I hadn't realised how lost I'd feel without him.

I had to stay strong.

Shaking my head, I pulled into Travis's driveway. The gates were closed. A man, different to the one I'd taken down, stood in the guard station. He came out when I stopped. I rolled down my window. "Violet Marcus."

The man nodded. "He's expecting you," he said, then walked back into the station and pressed the button for the gates to open. I slowly drove through. My whole body was on edge. Not knowing what the night would be like didn't sit right in my chest. My hands were even sweating.

But I was there for Izzy since she'd asked, okay, more like forced a dinner on me.

Then why did I have make-up on, my hair down, and a nice dress on?

For myself. I wanted to look nice for me. It had nothing to do with the man who stood in the open front door, leaning against the frame, dressed in jeans and a tee.

Jesus, he looked amazing in a suit, but in casual clothes, he was fantastic.

I opened my door, got out, and started for the house without glancing at him. I wanted to punch myself in the gut because I was already finding it hard to breathe. I wiped my hands on my dress and then brought my handbag strap back up on my shoulder when it started to fall.

"Evening," Travis said. His voice seemed deeper, rougher.

Sexier?

No, dammit.

"Hey." I nodded and looked over his shoulder. "Where's Izzy?"

"Upstairs. She'll be down in a second I'm sure." He stepped back, and I moved in. When the door closed, I jumped. Christ, I had to calm down. I wasn't sure where this jittery fool came from, but I refused to let her stay inside of me.

Only my body jolted when a hand touched my waist. Travis's warm breath caressed my cheek when he leaned down to whisper, "You look beautiful."

I cleared my throat, stepped out of his reach, and mumbled, "Yeah, well, um, I thought Izzy would like dresses, so I wore one." The front foyer was large. I glanced around again, giving myself something to do. "So where's Izzy?" Shit, had I already asked that?

When Travis chuckled, it told me I had. Thankfully, heavy footsteps sounded above, and I looked up in time to see Izzy bounding down the stairs. "You're here." She beamed.

Her smile was contagious. I grinned back just as wide. "I am, and I bought you something." She stopped just before me, bouncing up and down on her feet. I reached into my bag and pulled out the wrapped present. As soon as I handed it over, she plonked her butt down on the floor and tore at the paper.

"Wow. Daddy, look, look at what Miss Violet got me." She stood and thrust the present at her father. He grabbed it.

"That's very nice. Your bedroom will light up with fairies all over the walls at night now."

"It's the best thing in the world," she yelled, and then ran straight at me, her arms wrapping tightly around my thighs. She looked up, smiling. "Thank you."

My hardened heart cracked a little. Lifting my hand, I gently ran it over her head. "You're welcome."

"Izzy," someone called. I glanced up to see Link standing at the top of the stairs. "Come, and we'll put it in your room. You can show Miss Violet later."

"Yes. Can I, Daddy?"

"Go for it." He grinned down at her, then watched as she raced off. "You heading out?" he asked Link.

"As soon as I've done this."

"Thanks."

Link gave him a chin lift while smirking. Then he winked at me before disappearing down the hall upstairs.

"Is she always full of energy?"

"Yes." He chuckled. His hand dropped to my lower back. "Come into the kitchen with me. I'll grab you a drink."

"Sure." I nodded and started off to get away from his touch.

"Wrong way, Violet."

Damn it.

Pivoting around, I glared at him when he chuckled and followed him down the other hall beside the large stairs. Though, I wasn't sure following was a good idea. I should have raced ahead, so I didn't get to gaze at his butt in jeans. His butt always looked edible.

*All right, Violet. Harden the fuck up. Get over how good-looking that man is and get done with the night.*

I nodded to myself and then bit my bottom lip when Travis bent over in the fridge. But his arse.... *No, Violet. Don't remember how it felt in your hands when he buried—*

"Violet?" Travis stood, his lips twitching. He was trying to hide his smug smile but failed. I saw it and wanted to punch it off his face.

So what if he caught me staring at his arse. I didn't care.

Glaring, I asked, "What did you say?"

"Red or white wine?"

At the counter, I sat on one of the bar stools. "What do you think my answer will be?" He made out like he still knew me, but he didn't.

"Water," he answered.

Fuck him.

"Yes," I gritted out. Maybe he knew some small things about me. "So why did you ask what I wanted?"

He shrugged. "I had hoped you'd take me up on a drink because then I know you wouldn't drive home."

"And I wouldn't stay in your room if I did."

He snorted. "Of course not. Izzy is home. I do have multiple spare bedrooms."

"Water still. Thank you."

He nodded and got me a tall glass of water while he took a beer for himself. "Thank you again for coming to dinner. Izzy has been excited to see you."

My brows dipped, puzzled about why she would attach herself to me like that to begin with. "Does she often invite strange women to dinner?" The question popped out before I could swallow it down.

Travis's eyes narrowed. "No, she doesn't. Trisha is the only woman figure in her life. I didn't put her up to asking you, if that's what you're thinking. I'm also not having you here to replace anything you think may be missing from my daughter's life. As I said, Trisha helps take care of her when she can. If not Link."

"I didn't mean anything by the question, Travis. I was just surprised a little girl, who doesn't know me, would want to ask me to have dinner."

Someone cleared their throat. We turned to Link in the

doorway. "Izzy will be down in a second." He moved into the room and grabbed a phone off the counter. He faced me. "She talks about you." My body jolted back a step.

"What?" I whispered.

His head tilted towards Travis. "He won't tell you, but I will."

"Link," Travis growled out.

Link shook his head. "He keeps a photo of you in a frame in his office. Izzy told me about how she found it and asked her daddy who the lady was. He told her how he used to love you so much, but work got in the way, and he missed his chance at his happy ever after."

Stupid tears threatened, and my chest ached in a way I wasn't sure was healthy. I gripped the counter tightly.

"I think this is Izzy trying to give her dad his happy ever after."

"Goodbye, Link," Travis clipped.

Link scoffed. "Yeah, later you two. Be good for Izzy."

All I could do was nod stiffly as Link walked out quietly.

He'd missed his chance at a happy ever after.

With me.

He'd said that to his daughter.

That was how Izzy knew me, was comfortable inviting me over.

Damn him for the tears that dropped. I quickly stood and turned away, fisting my hands over and over. How dare Link tell me those things. How dare my heart react to those words. How dare my eyes leak as they were.

Damn it all.

I wouldn't cry. I didn't know why I felt like crying.

"Lettie," Travis whispered into the quiet room.

"Don't," I begged. I wasn't ready for any of this. I was still pissed about him tapping my phones, and his business. I wasn't ready to have my body fill with need.

A need for Travis.

No, I still refused to melt completely.

I swiped at my eyes, turned, grabbed my water and gulped it down. Clearing my throat, I asked, "What's for dinner?"

He ran a hand through his hair and sighed. "It's a roast."

He always liked cooking, even back when he lived in his shitty apartment with his crappy mates. He'd been the main cook for the household, and I did love going there for whatever he'd created. Thinking of it reminded me of the times we'd had alone in his apartment. Since I lived in an even bigger shithole, I loved going to his place when his roommates weren't there and pretending we lived in the apartment alone.

"Sounds and smells good."

He smiled softly. "It should be ready soon."

Travis saw me as his happy ever after.

Why?

Yes, we'd had an amazing relationship back in the day, but how could he still think that? Why would he tell his daughter that?

Pushing those thoughts aside, I took my seat again and nodded. "Um, this house is huge for just you and Izzy."

He chuckled as he checked the roast. "It is. But it reminded Izzy of a castle when we started looking. When her whole face lit up, I knew it was the one. We love the area, the peace to it, and I had hoped when Izzy starts school next year, she'll enjoy the country schools more than she would have the city ones."

"Does she go to kinder now?"

He leaned back into the bench and nodded. "She does. A few days a week. Trisha had already been living in Ballarat, so she helps with pickups and dropoffs when I'm busy with work. Though, I do try to do most of it."

I just bet the kinder teacher loved it when Travis went there.

My lower stomach burned.

I wouldn't admit it was jealousy.

"You have a beautiful daughter."

His eyes warmed. "I do."

We both looked towards the entryway when we heard the sound of tiny feet making a big slapping sound on the floor.

"Miss Violet," Izzy yelled, entering the kitchen. "You should see my room. There's fairies everywhere." She grabbed my hand and tugged on it. "Come look."

Travis chuckled. "How about you show her after dinner since it's ready?"

She pouted, and I would have given her everything, but then she smiled. "Okay, Daddy."

*Daddy.*

Travis was a father, and from what I learnt over sharing a meal with them, he was strict when needed, but other than that, he was the sweetest father, and she shone from his words, praises, and teasing. I honestly wasn't sure I'd enjoy myself, worried I'd be too wrapped up in my own head, but I was wrong. They made sure to include me in every conversation. Travis even teased me when I pushed the beans aside, reminding me how I used to do the same when we used to date, how he'd hoped I'd grown out of it.

I screwed my face up. "That's something I'll never grow out of."

"Does that mean I don't have to eat my beans?" Izzy asked.

Travis shook his head. "Eat four at least."

She groaned. So I tried suggesting, "How about we both suffer through it and eat just four."

Izzy nodded eagerly. We picked one up and shoved it in our

mouths. She didn't seem to gag like I wanted to, but I held it down for her. Travis, of course, knew this and laughed hard.

But then... God, then, since he knew I was struggling, he took the other three from my plate and then Izzy's and ate them for us. I wasn't sure why his actions thawed my heart just a little more, but it did.

He winked. Izzy clapped and giggled.

I smiled and laughed more in that night than I had in a long time.

# CHAPTER EIGHT

## TRAVIS

*I* could have killed Link for telling Violet about the photograph in my office. I was sure she'd run from the room scared. She hadn't. It had killed me to see the tears in her eyes, how her body shook, her hands fisted, but she'd stayed. I could have kissed Link instead.

After dinner, Izzy took Violet to her room to see the fairy lights Violet got her. That had shocked me as well. Violet bought Izzy a present. Knowing she'd thought of Izzy was sweet. While I knew my girl was amazing, I hadn't thought Izzy would manage to capture Violet so quickly, especially since Violet used to tell me she never wanted children.

Things could change.

Hopefully, they kept changing.

For her, for me, for us.

As I was coming from the hall near the staircase, I watched Izzy holding Violet's hand coming down the stairs. They were talking about something, well, mainly Izzy was, but Violet was grinning down at her. They were lost in each other and didn't even see me as Izzy guided Violet towards the living room.

Seeing their hands clutched together was... something beautiful.

Izzy didn't know her mother, and if I could, I would make sure it stayed that way. I wasn't interested in Violet as a replacement mother figure for Izzy. I was selfish and wanted Violet for myself, but seeing them interact with each other tightened my chest in the nicest way.

Walking into the living room, I spotted Izzy sitting on the couch and Violet on the floor in front of her. "I love your hair," Izzy commented.

"And I love yours."

"You can do mine after, if you want?"

"I'd enjoy that." She winced when Izzy pulled too hard. "Be sure to be gentle, Izzy."

They both looked over at me. "I will, Daddy."

My steps stopped when Violet smiled up at me.

She was smiling at me.

At the man who'd tapped her phones. I was a fucking idiot.

At the man who pimped women out.

Violet was smiling up at me.

It started to fade because I stood there staring at her like a goddamn fool. Quickly, I grinned back and then asked, "Would anyone like ice cream for dessert?"

"Me! Me, me, me," Izzy said, bouncing on the couch.

Violet glanced behind her, laughing. She looked back at me. "I guess I'll have some too, thanks."

Christ, I could picture this every night for the rest of my life. I wanted it to be true. I wanted Violet always at my side.

I had to make it happen.

Nodding, I said, "I better go get some before my princess turns into a monster."

"Daddy," Izzy whined. "I'll never be a monster."

"Sure, Izzy. Sure."

67

She cackled.

By the time I made it back in with a tray of bowls full of chocolate ice cream, it was to see Izzy holding Violet's head and shouting, "See, Miss Violet, that's Ariel. Isn't she beautooful?"

It looked like Izzy was teaching Violet all about princesses. Ariel was her favourite.

"I see, Izzy." Violet grinned.

Of course, when I noticed her hair in two pigtails on the top of her head, I started chuckling. "Nice hair, Lettie."

I didn't miss the way her body tensed, until Izzy started hugging Violet around her neck saying, "See, I told you Daddy would love it. He loves my hair like that."

Fuck me.

Violet's lips twitched. Then she laughed, her hands reaching up to pat Izzy's arms still around her neck. "I'm glad he likes it."

"Yay," Izzy cheered. Then she shouted, as if Violet couldn't see already, "Look, Daddy has ice cream."

"How about we forego the hairdos and eat while watching Ariel?"

"Yes," Izzy chimed in. "Come sit next to me, Miss Violet." She patted the spot next to her. Violet got up, which gave me a shot at staring at her arse, then sat next to Izzy on the couch waiting.

I handed out bowls, took the last one for myself, and then sat on Violet's other side. She didn't tense or glare at me. Instead, while she ate her ice cream, she asked Izzy questions about *The Little Mermaid*.

She seemed relaxed, even enjoying her night. For the life of me, I couldn't concentrate on the TV; instead, I watched the show beside me. Violet and Izzy.

"Miss Violet, do you work?"

"I do." Violet nodded. I reached for her empty bowl and put both Violet's and mine on the tray with Izzy's already finished bowl. "I work as a private investigator."

"Really?"

"Yes." Violet smiled.

"What does that mean?"

Violet laughed. "It means people come to me if they need help in finding something out, and I help them."

"Wow. That's cool. Daddy, I want to do what Miss Violet does."

Violet blanched. "It's not exactly safe." She was worried about my daughter.

Violet was worried about Izzy. Fuck, that felt good.

"That's okay," Izzy said. "I can so do it. We can work together when I grow up."

Violet hummed as she patted Izzy's hand on her arm and said, "We'll see how it goes when you're older."

"Yay!" Izzy sat back, her eyes went back to the TV, and she started singing off-key to one of the many songs on the show. Meanwhile, Violet looked to me, her eyes wide. I started laughing.

Leaning in, I whispered, "Don't worry, she'll change her mind like she does every other day."

"Okay," she whispered back, and went back to watching the movie, while I kept my eyes on Violet.

"Daddy," Izzy called.

"Yes?"

"You have to watch the movie, not Miss Violet."

Shit. I'd been caught and called out on it.

Violet's cheeks heated. "Yes, Travis. Watch the movie." Her lips fought a smile. She didn't seem annoyed I'd been watching her. I liked that.

"All right." I grinned.

It wasn't until the second movie about some rat cooking that I noticed Izzy yawning more and more. "Kiddo," I called.

"Yes, Daddy?"

"It's time for bed before you yawn your face off."

She giggled. "I can't yawn my face off."

"With the amount of yawning you have going on, I wouldn't be surprised. Say goodnight to Violet, princess, and I'll come up with you and get you into bed."

"But—"

"Izzy," I said.

Her mouth clamped closed. My daughter rolled her eyes and sighed. "Okay." She got to her knees, wrapped her arms around Violet's neck, while Violet hugged her back with her arms around Izzy's waist. "Night, night, Miss Violet."

"Goodnight, Izzy. I loved spending time with you."

Izzy pulled back. "You did?"

"Yes, honey."

Izzy beamed. "Yay. Means you'll come back. Right?"

"Of course I will."

Izzy leaned in, kissed Violet quickly on the cheek, and bounced off the couch. She made her way to the doorway. "Daddy, I'll see you up there."

"You will. Violet, would you like to stay longer or...." Her lips thinned and her eyes flashed wide for a moment before she controlled it. I left the choice up to her, unsure if she was ready to be alone with just me or if she wanted to run from the thought of just us alone in the room.

"I should get going."

Maybe she was scared to be alone with me... or scared of how her body would react if we were alone.

I smiled. "Princess, I'll just walk Violet to her car."

"Okay," she yelled, already headed out of the room. Violet stood and started for the door.

Standing, I followed her. She opened the door and went out. At least she didn't slam it, but rather, she left it open for me to come after her.

Violet stopped at the driver-side door. She turned, her hands playing with her dress. She fixed her bag on her shoulder, the one she'd left near the front door after giving Izzy her present. As I approached, she cleared her throat.

When a horn started honking, we both faced the gates. My phone rang in the next second. I pulled it out. "What?" I barked, just as Kathleen started yelling my name.

"Sir, Kathleen Stewart is at the gate."

"No shit," I answered. "Tell her I don't want to see her and call the police."

Violet's eyes darkened, her jaw clenching.

More honking and yelling.

"That's fucking it," Violet snapped. Her bag dropped to the ground, and she headed for the gates.

Ending the call, I quickly slipped my arm around her waist. "Stop. The police are on the way. She'll get taken in."

"And probably let out because she's not exactly on your property," she fumed.

"At least it could lead to her not showing her face here. She'll know we'll call the police from now on."

"The woman needs a good fist to the face."

"Until she tries to harm Izzy in any way, I won't let anything happen to her because she is, unfortunately, Izzy's mother. One day she could get clean and realise what a huge mistake she made when it comes to her daughter." It was what I'd always hoped for. It made me fucking ill knowing she'd chosen drugs over a decent life. And I knew drugs messed with her mind the night she'd accused her own daughter of being a monster. She hadn't meant to stab me. I saw the regret in her eyes when she'd been sober. I also saw the woman I'd cared

71

about at the start. So I kept trying to placate her for Izzy's sake, all for Izzy to have a relationship with her mother. A daughter needed a mother in her life. I glanced at Violet. Or a daughter needed a good female role model in her life.

"Do you honestly think that?"

"For Izzy's sake, I do hope so."

"You're a good man, Travis Stewart."

My fucking chest expanded at her comment.

"Daddy," came from behind us. I turned both of us, not wanting to release Violet to see Izzy standing on the steps above. "Is that my mummy?"

Violet went to her before I could. She swept Izzy up in her arms and took her inside. Protecting her. Christ, she thought I was a good man, but she was a better woman.

It was an hour later, after the police had taken Kathleen away and Violet had read to Izzy until she fell asleep, that Violet and I were once again standing outside near her car.

"Thanks for dinner." Violet smiled. "Izzy is amazing."

"She is," I agreed, stopping right in front of her. "Go on a date with me," I blurted.

Her body jolted, her wide eyes coming up and pinning me to my spot. "What?" she breathed.

"Go on a date with me... please."

"I don't think—"

"Did you enjoy tonight?"

"Yes."

"Did you suffer from my company?"

When she bit her bottom lip, my gut sank. Only then she whispered, "No."

My gut sprung back up to its rightful place. "Then you could like dinner with just the two of us."

She glanced to the side, thinking. "Maybe."

"I'll pick you up this Friday." It was a week away. Enough

time for more calls from me, more getting to know one another so she could become more relaxed. I hoped.

"Um… okay." She nodded, and I felt like whooping in joy.

She'd agreed to a date.

Progress.

Of course, I reached for more. "Can I kiss you goodnight?"

"No, yes. No." She opened her door quickly and slipped in. "Night," she said before slamming her door.

Hell, I didn't care. Even as I watched her drive away, I did it smiling because she'd said yes in between her two nos. I couldn't wait until our date where I may have a better chance of getting a firm yes from her.

Christ, my cock thickened. It liked the thought of that.

# CHAPTER NINE

## VIOLET

"You didn't tell me we'd be traveling to Melbourne for the date," I said, shifting in the passenger seat to stare at Travis. He looked amazing, like always. Damn him. He'd dressed in one of his expensive suits. Awareness hit me. Knowing where he got his money from curled my belly. I glanced away and pushed that thought down. I promised myself to be on my best behaviour, and I would. I knew it would be strange, maybe even difficult with only the two of us and no Izzy as a buffer, but I wanted to give this a shot because I enjoyed... no, I loved the side of Travis I saw when he was with his daughter.

"I said where I wanted to take you would be a surprise." He smiled.

My heart stumbled. I glanced away again. He *had* said he wanted it as a surprise on the phone earlier in the week when I asked multiple times where we'd be going. I didn't expect to be traveling out of town for it, and what if I wasn't dressed right for the date? I played with the hem on my black dress. Then again, it'd been said a little black dress could be for any occasion. I mentally berated myself for caring what I looked like. I had to stop.

He either accepted me as I was or not at all.

I had a feeling he would accept me even if I wore tracksuit pants and a sweater.

Travis wasn't shy about how he wanted me in his life. I knew it, and even though it scared the hell out of me because of his business, I was still in the car there with him.

And all because I had seen the man he was with Izzy, and I wanted to be around that man. A lot. Especially when he'd dealt with his ex in a way that showed him to be a better man than I realised he was. If it had been me, I would have used words and fists as my weapon, but he didn't do either. He stood back and let someone else deal with it because he had hope for Izzy and her mother to one day have a better relationship. He thought of Izzy before himself.

He amazed me.

Hell, all these feelings were after only one night of being around him.

What would tonight lead to then?

Having him alone could cause me to throw the differences between us to the wind and yell, "Fuck it," while falling into bed with him.

After all, he had asked me to pack a bag for the night. I did, with a promise to him over the phone that I wouldn't be sleeping with him.

If the night was as amazing as it had been at his place, though, my willpower would fall to the floor along with my clothes.

How crazy was that?

It was too soon, but I couldn't help but remember the days, years we'd had when we were younger. We'd been strong and real. After being around him, it was clear my feelings for him were still inside of me. They'd been buried over the years but had perked up at first sight of him.

Yes, this was crazy. We still had a long way to go if we ever wanted something like we'd had, but I did want to see how the night went.

The drive went fast as we spoke of random things during the trip. It wasn't until we sat in some fancy restaurant that I asked, "Tell me something I don't know about you."

"You already know I own an electronics company."

I rolled my eyes. "Don't remind me."

He chuckled. The waiter set down our drinks we'd ordered on arrival, and when he moved away, Travis said, "I also co-own a construction company with Link. Then there's the law firm I own."

"A law firm?"

"Yes." He smirked. "And I co-own a few branches of hair-dressing shops around Australia."

"Hairdressing?" I laughed. "How did that happen?"

"Link's sister wanted to run her own. I went into partner-ship with her."

"That's... nice."

He shrugged. "Link and I have been friends for a long time. When he refused to place his name to 'anything girly'—his words—Trisha came to me. She has a brain for it, so I backed her and it paid off."

"I like this," I blurted, feeling my cheeks burn.

He leaned in. "What?"

I licked my suddenly dry lips, glanced around, then returned my gaze to him. "Talking with you."

His eyes darkened. "Spending time with you is what I like."

"I know," I said, and both of us laughed.

We moved onto Izzy, what school she'd be going to, and if she would be doing out-of-school activities. I told Travis how I liked she had the support, not only from her father, but Link and Trisha also.

The night was running smoothly, and the more I looked at him, talked with him, and was just around him, the more it reminded me of the days before, in our past, and how comfortable I felt with him. My feelings grew throughout the night, causing me to feel lighter within myself. He made me laugh, smile, and even feel excited.

Of course, things didn't stay that way.

"Mr Stewart," was cooed close by. I tensed, already hating the sound of the needy voice.

Travis and I glanced to the side when two women stopped there.

"Lenore, Liza. What are you both doing here?" Travis asked pleasantly, though I could see his posture stiffen, his eyes harden.

"We're here with Mr Himmel," Lenore, the busty redhead, said.

Liza giggled and winked down at Travis. I clenched my jaw. My eyes widened when Lenore pulled out a chair and sat, while Liza got close to her back and ran a hand over Lenore's shoulder, flicking her hair off.

They were Travis's.

They had to be his employees.

I glanced over to the table Lenore pointed at before and saw a balding, overweight man in his fifties. He smiled, lifted his drink my way and winked.

I tuned back into the conversation to hear Liza say, "I remember that night explicitly. We had so much fun with you, Mr Stewart."

Travis chuckled.

I saw red.

Did he really just sit there, instead of telling them to fuck off, talking and flirting lightly with them?

Lenore's hand slid over the table. It landed on Travis's. I watched it, him, and my shoulders dropped, along with my stomach. My heart wasn't faring too well either because he didn't move his hand away.

He spoke with them like he cared what they had to say.

I guessed it was good for being employer and employee, but for me to witness it, to sit there on a fucking date and watch women pawn over Travis... it wasn't good at all.

He hadn't introduced me.

Hadn't acknowledged me since their arrival.

He wasn't the same man I shared a meal with. He wasn't the same man I watched with his daughter.

I didn't like the man in front of me.

Not at all.

This scene angered me to a point I clutched the steak knife in my hand. Disappointment at him, and at my reaction, raced through me. My brows dipped. Most of all, hurt spread through my chest and clogged my throat while tears threatened to fall.

Liza giggled. I imagined throwing the knife at her throat. Lenore hummed under her breath, her fingers stroking over Travis's hand. Both stared at him like they were hungry for dessert.

My stomach rolled.

Dinner threatened to come back up.

Enough was enough.

All eyes flashed to me when my knife, pointy side down, ended up in the table. "I'd like to leave," I said low.

Travis's jaw clenched. I didn't give a fuck if he was upset with me by my actions. I didn't give a fuck at all at that moment. I wanted out of there.

Travis nodded. He finally took his hand away from under

Lenore's. I caught his eyes widen a fraction, as if he was surprised by her hand on his.

Fucking bullshit.

How could he not know? I knew where my hands were, near ripping my handbag to shreds. I stood, as did Travis. His hand landed on my lower back, and I shifted away.

"Violet, I'd like you to meet—"

"I don't want to meet them," I snapped.

Liza huffed. "Rude."

"Ladies, if you'll excuse us, have an enjoyable night." He laid some money on the table, while the idiots giggled. I stormed off. He would follow, and I would wait for him and the car out the front. Then I would plan how to get back to Ballarat that night.

I wouldn't stay in a house with this man.

I couldn't be around him much longer.

"Violet," Travis called after me as I exited the restaurant. I heard him open the door, speak with the valet, and then I felt his heat at my back.

"It's not what—"

"Don't. Jesus, just don't."

"We'll talk at the house then?"

I nodded. That nod was a lie. We drove to the house in silence. Actually, it hadn't been a house at all, but an apartment. A very flashy apartment where there was a valet, a doorman, security, and once on the top floor, a large apartment. I noticed my overnight bag just inside the front door. I made a note to myself to grab it on the way out.

"I'll just take a shower and then we can talk."

I ground my teeth and nodded.

He walked off down a long hall. As soon as the door closed behind him, I took his keys off the table near the front door, grabbed my bag, and made my way back downstairs.

"Miss Marcus," the doorman called. Travis had introduced me when we'd arrived. Donald was a man in his sixties. He had a friendly smile and eyes that felt like they could read your thoughts.

"Is everything all right?" he asked, approaching me.

"Fine," I bit out. "Can someone bring Travis's car around?"

His eyebrows shot up. "But you just arrived, and usually Mr Stewart calls down for his car before he leaves."

Closing my eyes, I gripped the bag in front of me tighter. Opening my eyes, I held out the keys, my gaze to the floor. "Please, Donald." My fucking voice quivered.

My emotions were getting the better of me and soon I would be a blubbering mess, but I refused for it to happen there. They could wait until I was safely at home.

"Yes, Miss Marcus," Donald said softly, taking the keys from me. "You know, if you need a moment, I have a room out back that you could use."

Shaking my head, I said, "Thank you. But I need to get home."

His hand landed on my shoulder. "Of course." He quickly went outside to speak with the valet.

I was grateful I didn't have to wait too long. Donald returned. He ushered me outside and into the car. "Please drive safely."

"I will." I nodded, offering him a sad, watery smile.

"Take care, Miss Marcus."

"Violet," I called.

He smiled. "Violet."

Somehow, and I didn't know how exactly, I made it home and into my house before I fell to my bed and broke.

# CHAPTER TEN

## TRAVIS

*S*ighing, I punched the shower wall again. I'd fucked up. I knew I had, not only from Violet's silent treatment on the drive back to my Melbourne apartment, but because I'd acted like a fucking moron in front of her. Talking to my employees like they were something special to me. They weren't. But I had to make them feel they were so they did the best job they could. It had always been something I did. If they thought I treated them like diamonds, they would continue being an asset in my business.

It didn't help that I'd slept with both of them years ago—one stupid drunken night.

I'd royally fucked up big time and wouldn't blame Violet if she kicked me in the balls. I deserved it. I deserved worse.

Turning off the shower, I got out and grabbed my towel. I didn't bother drying myself. I had to go out there and beg for forgiveness.

I'd gone for a shower because I felt fucking dirty for the way I'd acted. I should have introduced her to them from the start, at least then, I may still have Violet talking to me, but I hadn't because I didn't want them to know anything about Violet. She wasn't a part of that world. She was good. Clean.

Christ, I hoped my time in the shower would also help Violet calm down a little. The drive to the apartment wouldn't have been enough for her to listen rationally to me.

However, I knew if the shoe were on the other foot, I'd be an absolute prick. I wanted her to yell, to scream at me. I didn't like the silence. Hell, I'd even suggest she could hit me a few times, or I'd do it myself.

Making my way into the room, I paused. No Violet.

I went from one room to another searching for her.

"Violet," I called, walking out of the last spare room, my stomach beginning to bottom out.

No answer.

"Violet?" I called again, heading for the living room. She wasn't there. I ran to the kitchen, the dining room, the games room, and the second living room. She wasn't in any of them.

It was then, as I made my way back near the front door, I noticed her bag was gone from the floor where the doorman had dropped it after I'd asked my driver to deliver it to my apartment.

Violet had left.

My heart hammered in my chest.

Fuck.

She'd left without wanting to see or hear me.

I couldn't blame her.

But it fucking killed.

I was in deeper shit than I thought.

"Fuck," I roared into the silent room. I stomped down the hall, headed into my room and then to my walk-in robe. Dropping the towel, I dressed in jeans and a T-shirt. I went to my bed, sat, opened my bedside table and pulled out some socks.

Only to stop.

I'd been ready to race after Violet and beg, but I wasn't sure it would work.

"Fucking hell," I muttered. I was a complete and utter goddamn idiot. I had Violet with me, on a date. We'd been talking, laughing, having a great time, and then I'd screwed it over.

I fucking messed it up.

My actions were pathetic. I may have just ruined my life, what I wanted most.

I threw the socks at the wall. Running my fingers through my hair, I cursed myself. I had to think of something to get her back.

I needed Violet in my life.

The time we'd had would never be enough. Two dates, one with Izzy around, which I absolutely classed as a date, and I'd fucked things up in a way I wasn't sure Violet would listen to me.

I wasn't sure Violet would accept my apology and give me a chance again.

I knew I didn't deserve it, but I had to try.

Violet was mine.

We had a past, and I wanted a future with her. Even after those short dates with her, I knew I was a total cockhead for letting her go, especially knowing she was meant to be mine. She hadn't changed as much as she thought she had. It was I who'd changed, and I didn't like myself for who I'd become. How I'd acted.

Rubbing at my chest, I cursed myself over and over again.

I had to find a way to convince her that what I did, how I acted, would never fucking happen again. Jesus, I would rather gut myself, cut out my own tongue, to ever see her face crumpled with disappointment and hurt again.

Stalking out of my room, I went to the table near the door, where my phone was, and picked it up.

First, I sent a text to Violet. **I'm sorry. I know it's not enough, but I am so fucking sorry for tonight. I know I ruined it. I know me explaining how it was only one drunken night many years ago with those two isn't enough for you to come back to me.**

**I'm sorry.**

**Truly sorry.**

**Christ, I just hope one day you'll forgive me. I'm not asking for it now when I know what happened was disgusting.**

**Shit. I'm terrible at expressing anything over text.**

**Need you to know, Violet. I won't give up.**

**I can't.**

Clenching my jaw, I read over what I'd sent and thought I sounded like a pathetic twat. I couldn't take any of it back; I'd already sent it without thinking. I wasn't sure if any of what I said would be any good at getting her back with me. But she had to know I regretted my actions.

I scrolled through my contacts, found Link's name, and hit Call.

"Yeah?" he answered.

"Need you here at the Melbourne apartment."

There was silence on the other end, and then, "I thought Violet was with you tonight."

"Fuck, Link."

"What the fuck did you do?"

"Just get here."

He hung up. I quickly dialled downstairs, already guessing how she left, but I needed to confirm it.

"Travis," Donald answered.

"Tell me how she left."

84

"In near tears and in your car."

"Fuck. Did you have someone tail her, make sure she got home safe?"

"I may be old, Travis, but I'm not stupid. She's the first I like for you." Donald had been working for me for years. He didn't have a family of his own, which was how he came with me wherever I moved to. In a way, like Izzy, Link, and Trisha, he was a part of my family.

"Thanks, Donald."

"You're welcome. I'll inform you when she makes it home."

I ended the call and threw my phone to the counter after walking into the kitchen and grabbed myself a straight bourbon. Sculling it back, I took the bottle and glass with me and went to wait in the living room.

I wasn't sure how long I sat there in a foul mood until I heard the front door bang open. I stood and made my way into the foyer.

"Rough night?" I asked, thanking fuck once more Donald was employed by me since Link showed up with his hands covered in blood.

"Let's just say Mr Sanders understood the message we delivered."

"Good," I clipped, tipping back my drink. Turning, I went back into the living room, knowing Link would clean up first and then head to find me. Mr Sanders was a top-paying client. Apparently, he considered I would look the other way if he got rough with my girls. He was mistaken. I didn't give a flying fuck about him or his money. My girls were to stay safe, no matter who the client was. If it wasn't me, then Link would ensure the clients understood the message clearly.

Link stomped in, stopped and crossed his arms over his chest. He glanced around. "Pity party for one?"

"Yes."

"What did you do?"

"Fucked up."

"How bad?"

"Bad enough she left while I was in the shower."

"Christ, Trav, tell me." His eyes narrowed. He came over and sat in the chair opposite me.

Leaning forward, I dropped my glass on the coffee table between us, ran a hand through my hair, and clenched my jaw. "Dinner was going great. Then I fucked it up when Lenore and Liza came over."

"No." He shook his head.

"Mr Himmel thought it was a good idea to take the girls out together. You know the goddamn usual. He shows off money, gets them wet from it. They saw me. Thought they'd pop over."

"They spoke shit in front of Vi?"

Vi. He was already giving her a nickname.

"Yes," I gritted through clenched teeth.

"You let them."

I threw out an arm. "What was I supposed to do? They were with a client. I had to be pleasant."

"They spoke about you and them in front of Vi?"

I nodded.

"You motherfucking idiot."

"What was I supposed—"

"Set them in their place," he yelled. "You're too soft on them. They're employees. They need to know not to fuck with you around others."

"You used to be with me at parties while they hung all over us."

"That's fucking different, and you know it. Violet wasn't around. You were only pining over her, but she was in another fucking country."

Standing, I paced. "I know I fucked up, Link. I don't need you on my case. I already hate myself enough."

"Good."

"What do I do?" I demanded. "I need her back."

"You love her?"

Stopping, I scowled down at him. "You know I do."

"Tell her, show her, woo the fuck outta her in ways you've never done."

Growling under my breath, I said, "I'm not sure that'll be enough." I dropped my head. Words wouldn't be enough; she needed to see. My head lifted.

"You have an idea?"

"I do."

"Are you going to bloody tell me?"

Looking at him, I asked, "How would you like to take over the business?"

His head jerked back. "The women?"

I nodded. "The women. It's time I put it aside. It was never going to be for me in the long run, not with Izzy being around. I'd like to make the move from it."

"Are you sure?"

I scoffed. "Link, you practically run the show anyway."

"I do. But can you stay away from it all?"

I stared at him. "For Violet, I can do anything."

He whistled. "Holy fuck, you actually do love her."

Rolling my eyes, I ignored him. "Call my lawyers in the morning, set up the contract. I'll be signing it over to you. Be sure to let all the clients and girls know."

"If the girls want to see you?"

"I don't give a fuck what they want. What happened tonight shouldn't have happened. They either accept you as their boss, or they go elsewhere. Make sure they know I'm not to be contacted about the changes either."

He grinned. "I will."

"Good. Right, I have a lot of kissing arse to do."

"Lucky it's a nice arse to kiss." When I snarled, his hands shot up. Laughing he said, "All yours, mate. All yours."

"Yes, she is."

# CHAPTER ELEVEN

## VIOLET

*I* sat at my desk thumbing through some paperwork, trying to figure out where to start, when the front door opened.

"What the fuck do you want?" Warden boomed.

My head shot up and I spotted Travis standing just inside the door. Why Warden was so protective, I didn't know. It wasn't like we sat down for coffee and chatted about our misfortunes. He didn't know Travis was a huge gaping arse-hole. Though, I was sure he'd learn if Travis didn't get out of my business.

"I've come to talk to Violet."

"Not happening, motherfucker," Warden warned. "You think I don't know you've done something? She don't talk about her life, but I fuckin' know when she's hurtin', and I don't fuckin' like it or you. Back the fuck up and get out."

"Violet, please listen to me."

Warden started for Travis. He slipped through the small gated-off area to block off the front reception and shoved Travis.

"Violet. Just a quick word," he pleaded, his eyes searching mine. I shook my head and looked back down at the paperwork.

I didn't want to hear his words. Him begging for forgiveness. If I did, I would forgive him, and where would that leave me in the long run? We'd be out again, his women would see him, approach him, and fawn all over him, while I stood there like I was nothing.

Maybe he didn't think to introduce me at the start because he just didn't want me in that part of his life.

Fuck no. I wouldn't make excuses for him.

In time, yeah, I would probably listen, but I was stubborn enough to not want it now.

The front door opened and Warden walked back in. I hadn't even heard them leave, too lost in my own thoughts.

"Thanks," I said, with a pathetic smile that wavered.

Warden grunted. He went to his desk and started to work again. That was it, no questions, nothing, but he had my back.

For that, I loved him like a brother.

When my phone rang, I glanced at the screen, ready to hit the Cancel button if I saw Travis's name, but it wasn't. Thinking of brothers, mine was calling.

"Talon."

"Why haven't we seen you? You're back in my life, Violet, you're not backin' out now."

Smiling, I told him, "I've been busy."

He snorted. "Busy? But you can still call my woman to check in on her. So call your brother every now and then to let me know you're doin' okay. Got it?"

"Got it," I whispered, my chest warming. My brother cared as much as I did for him, finally again.

After work, I decided to take my brother's advice. Knowing he would be with Zara at the hospital, I headed there. On the way to her private room, I quickly bought some flowers and chocolates from the store.

Knocking, I heard, "Enter," clipped. Shaking my head, I walked in. Talon stood beside Zara's bed with his arms crossed over his chest and a scowl on his face. Zara smiled warmly as Talon stalked towards me. He cupped the back of my head, leaned in and kissed my cheek. My heart stilled. "Good to see you. I'm goin' for a fuckin' coffee before I pull her outta that bed and tan her goddamn arse. Talk some sense into her."

He walked out. I glanced back to Zara and watched her roll her eyes. I made my way over, placing the flowers and chocolates on the rollaway table in front of her. "What's happening?" I asked.

Her arm came out, her fingers gesturing me closer.

Shit. Did she want a hug?

I didn't hug people.

However, for her, I would. Sighing, I leaned in and hugged her close. "How are you?"

"Better again since the last time you called."

I sat in the chair next to her bed. "You want to talk about my brother? As long as it's nothing sexual, I'll listen."

She smoothed out her sheet. "He wants to teach Pick a lesson. I don't want him to."

"Pick, as in the brother who betrayed Talon and his club for money?"

"Yes, but he also took a bullet for my brother and Julian." She lowered her voice. "He shot Vic to spare my family. He's proved to me he can be trusted."

Dragging my top teeth over my bottom lip, I had to think of a way to make Zara understand where my brother was coming from. Usually, over this type of situation, I wouldn't condone action if it wasn't legal.

Only, I knew now, in recent days, Talon's morals were

rock-solid to the core. His were about family and protecting them. If he didn't get his way on this, Talon could look weak to his brothers.

I tapped Zara's hand and then clasped my fingers together on her bed. "You were taken from him."

"I know, but—"

"No, Zara. You were taken from him and his brothers, which caused you anguish. Hell, not only you, but the kids, your brother, and Julian. His own brothers did this. Brothers he trusted. He can't let this slide by with a slap on the wrist. Not for him, but nor for the rest of Hawks either. If people know there'll be no retribution for what Pick did, it could lead to something like this happening again. I'm not talking just from within Hawks, but others who would have heard about it. Others who would want to cause Talon trouble. One day it might not be you they take. It could be just Maya on her own. People need to see Talon won't let anyone fuck with his family."

Zara's eyes glistened with tears. "Okay, Vi." She sniffed. "I hate it, I really do, but I understand it better than him just telling me he was going to beat the frig out of Pick." She sighed, rested her head back for a moment and then looked at me. "Now, tell me all about Travis. Have you seen him?"

It was my turn to roll my eyes.

Her hand landed on my arm. "I didn't notice before because your brother was pissing me off, but I see some sadness going on. What happened?"

I wasn't one to open up, but Zara always made me feel comfortable around her, wanting to—I inwardly cringed—"girl talk," so I told her everything that had happened. She sat silently listening until I finished.

"What are you going to do?"

I shrugged. "I don't know."

"Do you know what I think?"

Smirking, I asked, "What?"

"I think, in the end, when you're not angry, hurt, and wanting to kill him, you'll see how you really feel. Though I have a feeling you already know, but you're worried because being in a relationship is a scary thing. Especially when a child comes with it also." She smiled. "I also know you've never spoken about a guy in the time I've worked with you, until now. Travis has worked his way into your heart, again. You just have to figure out how you want to deal with it. I'm sure he's willing to wait while you do."

"I'm not sure."

She slapped my arm, and I glared up at her. "He'll wait because he sees something special in you."

Thankfully, before things got too mushy, Talon walked back in. Zara blurted, "I understand. Do what you have to do."

The scowl lifted, his eyes widening as he glanced to me. After a chin lift to me, he smiled warmly at his girlfriend. "Kitten," he said softly, and Zara got a dazed look in her eyes.

"I do love staring at your cute butt, boss man, but I'd like to get by to see my pumpkin pie," we heard from behind Talon. He shifted in, and Julian walked through, along with Deanna. I stood.

"My time to go," I announced and received an air kiss from Julian and a middle finger from Deanna, which I returned as I fought a smile. It was good to be around real people. Without thoughts of Travis or my emotions getting the better of me, I almost felt normal for a moment there.

Later that night when I arrived home, after surveying my neighbourhood to make sure Travis wasn't around, I found another delivery on my front porch. More flowers, some chocolates, and a small box.

Sighing, I unlocked and opened my front door. Picking up the items, I struggled through the entryway, since the bouquet was monstrous. I made my way to the kitchen, opened the bin and threw the flowers in.

The chocolates I would keep since they were my favourite. The box I sat on the counter and went about getting a whisky. My eyes kept drifting to the box not far from me. It taunted me, wanting me to open it. Frowning, I took a sip of my drink while glaring at the box.

It would get the better of me. I knew it would. *I may as well open it.* It would probably be more jewellery. I wasn't sure what Travis was thinking sending me all this shit. He couldn't buy my forgiveness. I made sure to collect all the jewellery in a pile near the front door. I was going to mail it back as soon as he stopped trying.

Would he stop?

He'd have to once he knew I wouldn't be bought from shiny things.

I grabbed the box and pulled it towards me. Undoing the bow, I lifted the lid.

Sucking in a sharp breath, my hands shook, my eyes widening.

He'd kept it.

All this time, he'd kept it.

The box was new, but what was in it wasn't.

I pulled out the first photo.

It was of us, on our first date back in university. My hand was over my mouth. Water slipped through my fingers because Travis had just said some corny pickup line, and I'd just taken a drink and about sprayed the whole table with it. Travis looked down at me smiling widely.

My heart skipped a beat taking in the image.

The next photo was of us at the park. We'd skipped class to relax on a rug with beer and Cheetos. We were lying back, and Travis took the photo as he leaned over to kiss my cheek.

My chest warmed.

The next photo was of me. I stood with my hands on my hips and a pissed-off look on my face. Laughing, I shook my head as tears threatened. Travis always took me at my worst, when my temper got the better of me. I'd been pissed because he got pineapple on the pizza; that was all it took to set me off. He'd told me, when he showed me the photo, he loved looking at it because no matter what mood I was in, he still wanted me.

My bottom lip trembled.

The following photo was of us that someone else had taken. I couldn't remember who, but I remembered that night. We stood on the dance floor in some club. People around us had been dancing crazy while Travis and I just held each other, swaying to the music and gazing into each other's eyes.

It was that night he told me he loved me.

That night we didn't fuck. We'd gone slow and made love to one another.

It was that night I knew I never wanted to live without him.

Only a year later, our lives changed. But I knew now it was for the better we'd gone our separate ways. I wouldn't be where I was today, and Travis wouldn't have had Izzy.

There was another photo of us hugging at a picnic bench. One, which someone else took, of us fighting outside a stadium. He hadn't liked it when I punched a guy for coming onto me since it was apparently his duty to take care of me. My anger hadn't lasted long. How could it when he wanted to be the one to protect me? I wasn't used to that from another man other than my brother.

So many photos, so many memories flashed through my mind.

We had been completely in love with each other.

It was no wonder my emotions were stronger in just a few weeks since being around him.

It was also no wonder I hurt the way I did.

Never had Travis paid another woman attention if I was around. I had to remember people changed.

She had been his employee, but I couldn't get the way they talked, the way they looked at one another, nor the way he let her touch him in front of me out of my mind.

Sniffing, I shoved the photos away.

*Damn him for this.*

Damn him for making me remember what we'd had.

The love we'd felt.

*Damn him.*

I didn't know what to do about this, what to feel. What I did know was that I still wasn't ready to see or talk to him.

I was probably holding a grudge, protecting myself from more hurt, but I couldn't stop. I wasn't ready.

Maybe with time, I would be.

Only, would Travis still be around then?

I jolted when my phone rang. At first, I didn't want to look to see if it was Travis, but Chuck was out with Butch on a case, and I had to make sure it wasn't either of them.

That was what I told myself when I reached for it.

It wasn't anyone I thought it would be. "Jim," I said when answering.

"Violet. Long time no talk."

It had been. Jim and I used to date before he left to see what city life was like in the police force instead of the country. Sometimes when I took cases out of town, Jim and I would catch up for a quick fix. We weren't serious, but we liked each other enough to sleep with one another. "How are you?" I asked.

"Good, honey. Coming to town in a few weeks, would love to catch up. Want to do dinner?"

Did I?

Jim was great to talk to. I had always enjoyed his company. "Sure. I'd like that."

# CHAPTER TWELVE

## TRAVIS

*I* really should have expected the visit. Still, the day after I went into Violet's office, I walked into my kitchen from my office, not expecting to see Talon sitting calmly at the dinner table. I stopped for a second, then casually continued to the fridge.

"Can I get you anything to drink?" I asked, taking out a beer for myself. He didn't answer, so I closed the fridge door. Turning, I leaned against the bench. "Are my men still alive?"

"The brothers are out there." He shrugged. "They could be."

My jaw clenched. It was fucking hard to find good men to work for me. Obviously I needed some skilled ninjas to deal with people coming into my house uninvited.

"What are you after, Talon?"

He stood, walked around the table and headed my way. I refused to move, to be intimidated. He stopped just before me, his eyes as hard as steel. "Warden called."

Fuck.

"I told you to stay the fuck away from my sister."

"She's been a big part of my life, and if I have my way, she will be again."

A muscle ticked his forehead. "From what I get, she don't want anythin' to do with you."

Straightening, I put my beer down on the counter behind me. "She's angry, upset, and hurt. I fucked up, I know I did, but I *will* prove to her we're meant for each other."

His face contorted into a fierce scowl. "She's upset? Hurt?" he demanded on a snarl. "What the fuck you do to her?"

"It's between Violet and me," I told him.

"Wrong." I didn't move despite knowing what was coming. When his fist connected to my face, I rocked to the side and straightened again. He got close. "You fuckin' go near her, you'll have more than just my fuckin' fist in your face."

"Lies," I hissed. "Or you would have killed me by now. You fear your sister disowning you if you harm me." I snatched my beer up and took a drink. Stepping away from Talon, I gave him my back, knowing I was right. He wouldn't kill me because he loved his sister, and he knew I loved her. "You've had your hit, Talon. The only reason *I* allowed it was because *I* felt *I* deserved it for hurting her. You can fucking leave now."

The front door opened, and little footsteps sounded on the hardwood floor. "Daddy!" Izzy called. She came running around the corner and skidded to a stop. "What happened to your face?"

Smiling, I forced a laugh. "Silly me tripped over and hit it."

She giggled. "Daddy, you have to be more careful. Who are all the big men outside, Daddy?"

Talon must have stepped out from behind me as Izzy's eyes widened. "Who're you?"

"They're my men, and I'm Talon Marcus."

Her head tilted to the side. "Miss Violet's last name is Marcus."

Link walked around the corner, gun in his hand. I shook my head at him, and he quickly put it away.

"She's my sister."

Izzy beamed. "Really? Cool, I love Miss Violet. She let me do her hair and brought me a fairy light for my room. But she's been too busy with work to come back yet. Next time I wanna watch *Beauty and the Beast* with her."

Talon nodded. "I'm sure she'll love that."

Izzy clapped. Link stepped closer to her and placed a hand on her shoulder. "What do you need to do when you get home, sweetheart?"

She sighed and rolled her eyes up to look at Link. "Take my things to my room and unpack them."

"That's right. Come on. I'll help."

"Okay. Bye, Mr Marcus."

"Later, squirt."

She giggled and waved. They went out of the room, but then I heard her run back in. "Almost forgot." She came at me. I crouched enough for her to plant a kiss on my cheek. "Hi, Daddy."

Chuckling, I kissed her cheek. "Hi, princess. Have a good day at kinder?"

"Sure did. I'll bring down all my drawings."

"Can't wait to see them."

As soon as she left, Talon turned to me. "That's also a reason I won't kill you. But you fuck my sister over, I'll second-guess my decision."

I nodded. Couldn't say I blamed him for the threat, but I wouldn't allow myself to fuck Violet over ever again. I just had to make her see that.

It had been nearly a month since seeing Violet. Since I fucked everything up. A month where she had evaded my texts, my calls, my emails, and my stop-ins. I'd thought something would have changed after the gifts or at the very least after sending her the photos. I'd hoped she'd remember how good we'd been together.

But there'd been no contact on her part.

It fucking scared me.

Still, I wouldn't give the hell up.

Patience was my new friend. One I'd never had before but was willing to give it a go for her.

Warden was like her personal guard, stuck to her like glue at work. He wouldn't let me pass, no matter how many times I tried.

I didn't want to shout out how I'd changed my life because of her. How better off I was with her in my days. I just needed a moment with her to let her know everything.

"Daddy," Izzy, in a tired voice, said from her bed after I'd started for the door.

Turning, I asked, "Yes, princess?"

"When will we get to see Miss Violet again?"

Fuck. She's been asking nearly every day, and all I had to tell her was soon, that Violet was too busy with work right now. I hated the way the lie tasted on my tongue. I couldn't exactly tell her it was my fault Violet wasn't around. I'd fucked up. Let business get in the way when I should have taken Violet into account right from the start.

"Soon, I hope, Izzy."

"Daddy?"

"Yes, sweetheart."

"Do you think Miss Violet doesn't like me, just like Mummy doesn't?"

A hand closed around my heart and squeezed.

Striding to the bed, I pulled back her covers and picked her up, holding her close. "Why do you say that, princess? Why do you think your mum doesn't like you?"

Her tiny arms wound around my neck, and she buried her head into my shoulder.

"B-because Mummy said so."

My body locked. I stared up at the camera in the corner of the room. Link was in the office waiting to go over some paperwork with me. I hoped to fucking Christ he was either listening or recording this for proof.

"When?" I managed to get out through my clenched teeth.

She sniffed. "S-she came to kinder, at the fence. She told me it was my fault you didn't love her. S-she said she hated me a-and wanted me gone."

Fucking hell. Jesus motherfucking Christ.

I cleared my thick throat. "Gone?"

"D-dead, Daddy." I could hear the tears in her voice.

I gripped her tighter to me. "Baby, princess... my sweet Izzy. Your mum's sick. She doesn't know what she says, but I want you to know you'll never see her again."

"I-is it bad I don't want to?"

"No, princess, it's not bad at all." I sat on her bed, laid her down, and I lay next to her, tucking her hair behind her ear. "Miss Violet would never, ever hate you, Izzy. She cares a great deal for you. I promise."

At least I knew that was certain.

"Okay, Daddy." She yawned, wiping at her tears.

"How about I lay here until you fall asleep."

"Yes."

"You know I'd never let anything happen to you, right, Izzy?"

Her smile settled me just a little, though anger still burned deep. She curled into me, her hand resting on mine over my chest. "I know, Daddy."

It took a little while for my girl to drift off. I'd read to her, told her stories of Violet since she wanted to hear some.

Finally asleep, I kissed her cheek and quietly walked out.

My phone rang as I walked down the hall. When I saw Trisha's name pop up, I quickly pushed my anger down and answered it. "Trisha, everything all right?"

"Anton and I are out to dinner," she whispered into the phone.

"Is there trouble? Do you need help?" Briefly, I wondered why she was calling me and not her brother. Either way, if she needed us to kick someone's arse, we would. Then again, she was with her husband and since he was a boxer, I would think he'd take care of any situation.

"No, it's great.... Look, it's nothing like that. Ah...."

"Trisha, what is it then?"

"It's Violet. She's also on a date at the same place."

"Where?" I snarled into the phone. I took the stairs two at a time on the way down, heading for my office. Trisha rattled off the place. "I'll be there shortly," I said, and hung up. I stalked into the office.

Link looked over. "I'll send the recording to the right people. Make sure she's in custody by morning."

"So you did get it?"

"Fuck yes."

"Good." I nodded. "You'll need to get a message to her somehow."

"I know a few birds on the inside," Link said.

"She needs to know if she ever gets out and shows her face to me or anyone in my family, she'll find a fucking bullet between the eyes." Even though I wanted her in pain, even killed now, I'd rather her rot in jail and live her days in hell.

"Done," Link bit out; he was just as furious as I was.

At my desk, I pulled the drawer open and snatched up my keys. "I have to go out. Will you stay for Izzy?"

"Yeah, mate. Never need to ask. But where you goin'?"

"I just got a call from your sister. She happened to see someone on a date."

His eyes flared. "Do I need to ask who?"

"Violet," I clipped roughly.

"Fuck."

"Exactly." I stormed out of the office and made my way to the front door.

"Just don't kill the bastard," Link called.

I couldn't promise that. I was already in a foul mood.

### VIOLET

It was easy to spot Jim through the restaurant since he was standing and waving me over to the table. Smiling, I made my way there. He'd wanted to pick me up from my place, but I told him I could be late since I was on a case.

"Vi," he murmured against my cheek after I'd reached his side, and he'd leaned in for a quick kiss on the cheek.

"It's great to see you, Jim."

"You too, honey." He pulled out my chair. I sat down, and he helped me push it back in.

"Tell me, how's the city?"

He groaned. "Terrible idea going from the country to the city. The people are crazier."

I laughed. "I tried to tell you that."

"You did." The waiter arrived, and we gave our order of

drinks. When he left our table, Jim announced, "I'm moving back."

My eyes widened. "You are?"

"Yeah, honey. Had enough. Give me the country any day."

"When's the move? Do you need help?"

He smiled softly. "Already done. I shifted last weekend. Now tell me what's been happening with you."

God, a lot of things and yet so little too.

Travis.

No, I wouldn't think of him. He'd already plagued my mind constantly, and I'd lost count of the times I'd looked at those photos. It was exactly the reason why he'd sent them.

He'd screwed up, yes.

Though I may have held my grudge a little too long. The only thing was, I wasn't sure if we could have a future.

Deep down, I wished it was possible, but I was scared of the unknown.

The waiter dropped our drinks to the table. I quickly looked at the menu since Jim already knew what he wanted when I'd asked. After ordering and we were alone again, I told him, "Nothing really, just busy with work. Chuck's leaving next week, so we've been training a new guy. His name's Butch."

"Chuck, Butch," he said with a chuckle. "Where do you find these guys?"

Smiling, I shrugged. "They find me."

"How's Warden?"

"He's doing well. Now, since I know you're coming back to the country force, do you mind if I run something by you?"

He grinned. "It wouldn't be the same if you didn't. Hit me."

We talked about a couple of cases I was on while we drank, waited for dinner, and as we ate. I forgot how lost I could get in work and talking about it with someone who knew the line of business.

Sitting back, I rubbed my stomach. "I'm so full, and I've done enough talking about business. Tell me, are you moving back with someone special?"

Jim smirked. "You know I wouldn't have asked you here if I was."

"But we're friends, right? Even if you had been dating, engaged, or married, we'd still be friends."

He winced. "Friends." He leaned into the table. "I had been hoping you'd say more."

I thinned my lips, staring at him. "I... um, my... life in that area is complicated."

He hummed under his breath. "So this was just a catch up between friends in your books?"

It was my turn to wince. I hated I hadn't been direct to begin with. "I'm sorry."

Jim shook his head. "No need to apologise, honey. I do love talking to you."

"Same with you." I smiled. My eyes drifted over his shoulder and widened.

"Violet?" Jim asked.

He went to glance where I had, but it was too late.

Travis already stepped up beside our table. He reached to the chair behind him and pulled it over before sitting down.

"Ah, are you all right?" Jim asked.

"No," Travis clipped darkly. His attention was solely on me, completely ignoring Jim. He reached out and took my hand in both of his. My heart jumped. I tried to pull away, but then he started talking, and I stopped moving, and I think breathing. "I love how your hair is so black that in the light it looks blue. I love it when you're happy, smiling, teasing. I also love it when you get pissed and angry and want to kick me in the face. I love your smile, your eyes, your body, your heart. I loved you back in university, Violet Marcus, and I still love you to this day. I can't imagine my life without you in it, and I don't wish to. We've already had too many years apart. I'm not willing to lose any more time without you in my days." Tears threatened, and my chest rose and fell rapidly. Still, he went on, "What happened will never, and I fucking mean goddamn never, happen again. The business is gone—"

I gasped. "Travis."

"I don't and will never deal with hookers again. I've handed the business over."

"Travis fucking Stewart," Jim said, shock and awe in his voice.

Travis once more ignored him, but I worried Jim was putting two and two together and knew exactly who Travis was in the underworld. The biggest pimp in Victoria. From the cunning look in Jim's eyes, it told me he had.

"Travis, you should—"

"Lettie," he said softly. "Please, let me make it up to you."

Jim started laughing as he stood. I pulled my hand away from Travis while he was distracted, watching Jim with a scowl.

Annoyance boiled my blood and yet it cooled, then warmed, and bloody felt like it swirled throughout me over Travis's words and his action of showing up here in the first place. Still, I focussed on Jim. "Jim, stay, you—"

Jim shook his head. "Honey." Travis cursed low. "Relax," Jim offered. "Vi, good luck with this one and your future. I already know I can't compete with him."

Wait, what? It was true…. No, I wouldn't admit that just yet, but Jim didn't have to give in so easily. "No, it's—"

Jim's hand came up. "We'll talk soon." His gaze drifted to Travis. "I know who you are."

Travis clipped back, "And I know who you are, Jim Binton."

Jim's brows raised. He snorted. "I'll be keeping an eye on you. Make sure what you'd said stays true. If you're out of the business, then we won't have a problem. If you're not, then... well, you'll see." He tapped the table twice. "Any chance you want to tell me who the new owner is?"

Travis's upper lip raised. "You fucking seriously asking me that?"

Jim's lips twitched, just like mine wanted to. It seemed Jim had bigger balls than I thought. "Worth a try." His face turned serious as he leaned in a little and said, "Just think yourself lucky it's Violet you're wanting, or I'd be hauling your arse so fast to the station you'd shit yourself."

Travis chuckled roughly. "You must be mistaken, Jim. Because I just don't give a shit what—"

"Enough," I snapped, glancing around.

Jim stood tall, his gaze came back to me. "Talk soon."

"Yes." I nodded. Nerves fluttered my stomach, knowing I was about to be alone with Travis.

# CHAPTER THIRTEEN

## VIOLET

*J*im walked out after stating he would be getting the bill. I didn't know what to say to Travis. I still couldn't believe Travis said what he did knowing Jim was a police officer. I also couldn't comprehend Travis giving up the business to begin with. For me.

Guilt swept through me.

Needing to centre myself, I took a sip of my drink. "You shouldn't give something up for someone."

My stomach was in a spin, along with my head, and my heart hadn't stopped its hard beat since he'd arrived.

Travis shook his head. "If it's for the right person, then you'd be willing to do anything."

Dear Jesus, Mary, and Joseph.

"You know my life. How my mother was a drunk and didn't give a fuck about my sister or me. How my sister hated me because I refused to get her the drugs she wanted."

I did know this. I just didn't understand where he was going with it.

"It was a year after we parted when I learned my sister, my

*own* sister, took up prostituting to make money for the drugs she was hooked on." I gasped, my hand flew to cover my rapidly beating heart. "I went looking for her, to try and help get her clean once and for all. But I was too late. She died in a hospital bed after her pimp, the man who was supposed to protect her the most, beat and raped her because she wouldn't take on certain clients." Tears welled in my eyes for his loss. "It was then I took over *his* business."

I knew what he meant by that. He'd killed the man who ended his sister's life, and I could never hate him for it.

He tapped his chest. "I chose to clean the business up. Got the women who wanted to leave out and made sure they would be content in life until they could find other employment. Those who wanted to stay, who liked the work they provided for the money they got, I made sure they were protected. The money that's made goes to the women. The only cut I take is to pay for their security. I have other businesses. I didn't need anything from this one. I did it because the women were treated poorly and I could help. So I did. So none of them ended up like my sister."

He'd told me, in front of Jim, he loved me. I couldn't understand it, but really in my eyes alone, he not only took up being a pimp for the right reasons, but he was giving it up for *me*. He couldn't imagine his life without me in it.

What did I do with all this information?

I couldn't think. I couldn't.... I didn't know what I couldn't do because I was lost in emotions swarming through my whole body and head.

He'd seeped his way into my life, but then hurt me. Did I take the leap of faith from what I was feeling in that moment? I cared for him too much, yet I was still scared it wouldn't work out.

I wanted to throw myself in his arms, but fear had me

holding myself still. When I didn't react, Travis sighed. He nodded. "I have to go."

"Okay," I whispered.

His eyes shone in what I thought was pain and worry. "You'll probably hear about it soon, but I want you to know from me. Izzy made a revelation tonight about her mother. She went to Izzy's kinder and told her she blamed our daughter for our breakup. That she wanted her dead."

I gasped. My hands clenched. "Is Izzy—"

"She's okay. I just need to make sure to be there tonight."

"Of course."

"Will you talk with me tomorrow?"

I hesitated and his jaw clenched. "Yes," I said.

He relaxed a little, and then stood. His hand steeled on my shoulder and applied a small amount of pressure. Then he was gone.

I made my way home with a mixture of feelings. Anger over what happened to Izzy raced through me. How fucking dare her mother say that to such a precious little girl.

That was another reason I had to be sure about where Travis and I would go in the future. Izzy. I had to take her into account. She may not want me with her father. The last thing I wanted to do was start something with Travis and settle down for it all to go to shit. Izzy'd had enough heartache. I refused to be the one to give her more.

Walking through my door, I went straight into my room and changed out of my dress into my sleeping clothes.

Sitting back on my bed, I pulled my legs up and hugged them to my chest.

What did I want?

Travis.

Izzy.

Them, in my life.

But I was scared.

So fucking scared it wouldn't work out, and I'd hurt not only Travis but Izzy as well.

Was it worth a risk?

Could I really be Travis's happy ever after?

He'd said he loved me with my temper, and he'd proved it enough when we were younger, but I could be a real grudge-holding bitch.

Yet, I still got over him tapping my phone to go on a date with him.

I also got over the episode at the restaurant.

But what happened if I didn't take a chance and I lost them forever?

Was I willing to risk that?

Sleep had been hard to come that night. I slowly blinked my eyes open to the morning light shining through the cracks of my blinds. My eyes were gritty, my mouth dry, and my head pounded. All of it told me I didn't get enough sleep since I couldn't shut my mind down.

Groaning, I threw back the blankets, knowing it wouldn't do any good lying about. I got out of bed and headed straight for the bathroom. After a long hot shower, I dressed in another set of jeans and a tee. Just after I managed my first sip of coffee, my phone rang.

I raced to my bag by the front door, thinking it could be Travis and realising I actually wanted to hear his voice. It wasn't.

"Jim," I answered, making my way back into the kitchen.

"Vi, how'd it go last night?"

"He left. Then I left. Look, I wanted to apologise—"

"You don't have to."

"Yes, I do."

"Honey." He chuckled. "I'll never see you look at me like the way you did *him*. I don't fucking trust the douche, but when it comes to you, and it kills me a little inside to say this, but I know he'd do anything in his power to make sure you're happy and safe because it's what I'd do if I had your interest like that."

Travis would.

God, he really would.

My throat thickened, and I sucked in an uneven breath. "But—"

"No buts, Vi. Understand the bastard gave up his *illegal* business for you. Someone must have tipped him off that you were out with me and he came to stop it. The schmuck doesn't want to lose you from his life. Fuck, even as a man I can admit not many men would do that for a woman."

He was right. Not many would.

Travis loved me.

Me.

Hot-headed, pain-in-the-arse me.

"I can't believe I'm even suggesting this, but fuck...." It sounded like he coughed and maybe even gagged a little. "You need to give him a chance, honey. Because if a woman looked at me the way you were with him, I'd think I'd won the damn lottery. Not sure what happened between you two, but, Christ, is it worth walking away from?"

"No," I whispered.

"Just make sure we stay in contact. Despite the prick you like, I still want to have you in my life."

I laughed. "I'll make sure of it."

"Take care, honey."

"You too, Jim, and thank you."

He didn't say anything back. The line went dead, and my

mind was finally clear.

I didn't want to lose Travis.

Sculling back my coffee, I grabbed an apple and bit down while I walked around collecting my phone, keys, and bag by the front door on my way out.

Travis wanted to talk. I hoped he meant whenever because I was about to pop into his place. On the drive, I quickly rang Warden.

"Yeah?" he said, picking up the phone.

"I won't be in for some time."

"You good?"

"Yes, ah, I just have to go see Travis."

Silence.

"Warden?"

"It's on again?"

"Yes."

"He fucks with you, I'll break him."

Smiling, I shook my head. "Nobody will fuck with anybody."

"See you when you get here," he said, ending the call. I noticed he didn't agree with me.

As I pulled up to the gate, the guard didn't even walk out of his station. Instead, he gave me a chin lift and pressed the button. The gates swung open a moment later. I must have been given an open invitation.

Once parked just near the front of the house, I got out and went to the front door. It swung open before I had to knock. Travis stood in it wearing jeans, a black tee, and his feet were bare.

"Violet, is everything all right?"

My gaze drifted back up to his face. Blood pumped faster throughout my body. I was near dizzy standing in front of him, knowing I was about to commit to this, us. "Yes." I nodded.

He studied me, his brows dipping in confusion. "Did you want to come in?"

Without a reply, I stepped closer. He moved out of the doorway. "Is Izzy home?" I asked. It had been so long since I'd seen her, I'd missed her a great deal.

"She is. She's upstairs with Trisha getting dressed. They're about to head out. Trisha's taking her to the salon to do her hair."

Smiling, I said, "That's sweet."

"It is." He nodded, his lips thinning, probably wondering if my being there was good or bad.

"Is her mother in custody?"

"Yes," he clipped. "I spoke to my lawyer. He thinks she'll be away for a long time since I reported that first incident and got what Izzy told me on tape."

"Thank God."

"I know."

"Still, it doesn't feel enough for upsetting Izzy."

His lips twitched. "My line of thought as well. However, I'm sure her stay won't be pleasant."

Meaning, he probably knew people on the inside and his ex was about to get in a shitload of trouble. "Good," I stated, and it was good. Izzy was only five. No child should hear those words from a parent.

"Miss Violet," was screamed from above.

Smiling, I watched Izzy race down the stairs. My heart skipped a beat when she nearly fell, and I started for her. She righted, kept coming, and threw herself at me on the last step. I wrapped my arms around her and swung her about.

"Izzy," I whispered into her hair. "I missed you."

She pulled back. "You did?"

"Of course."

She hugged me tighter. In my shoulder, she asked, "Will I

get to see more of you?"

I lifted my eyes from the floor to meet Travis's worried gaze. Was he worried about what my answer would be?

"I would like that."

"Yay, Miss Violet."

"Honey, you can call me Lettie."

Travis's tense body relaxed, his smile glorious. He ran a hand over his face and through his hair; it seemed he couldn't believe what he was hearing. I wanted to laugh because I felt giddy happy.

I then told Izzy, "Only the people who are special to me get to do that."

I heard a sniffle. "Lettie," she whispered.

A smiling Trisha stepped up to my side. "Come on, pumpernickel. It's time to do your hair."

Izzy pulled her face up. "But, Lettie's here."

"How about I promise to still be here when you get back?"

Travis's eyes flashed with delight on hearing that, causing my own smile to brighten more. I liked shocking him, making him happy.

"Okay." Izzy nodded, and I popped her back onto her feet. She gave me a quick hug around my thighs and then turned to her father. "Did you hear that, Daddy? Miss..." She glanced to me grinning. "I mean, Lettie is staying here until I come home."

"I did, princess. You have fun with Trisha and be a good girl."

"I will." She went over to him. He bent enough for her to kiss his cheek and she returned the gesture. "Bye, see you both soon." She took Trisha's hand and waved from the front door. I waved back, my heart in my throat seeing her so happy, and also the feel of Travis stepping so close, his warmth touching my back. Only his hands didn't, and I wanted them to.

Izzy hadn't been the only one I'd missed.

Of course, I'd missed Travis.

Not only with my heart, but my body and soul. It sounded ridiculous. But since my mind cleared and I knew what I wanted, I would take it.

As soon as the front door closed behind them, I faced Travis. His gaze was already down on me. Waiting, watching, and ready to listen to whatever I had to say.

"A chance," I said.

His eyes widened. "With me?"

"Yes. But I'm scared, Travis. Scared to hurt, scared to give this a try because if it doesn't work out, I'll have myself to blame, but it'll also be bad for not only us two, but Izzy."

"It'll work," he growled low.

"You want me, after everything? My grudge holding, my temper, my—"

His hands flashed out, wrapped around my waist, and dragged me into him. I placed my palms on his chest. He told me, "I'll always want you, and pray it'll be the same for you."

"I have an inkling I will."

"Fuck, Lettie."

"What?"

"You're here, in my damn arms, taking a chance on me."

"And you're taking a chance on me."

He leaned in, and in the next second, his mouth was on mine. He tasted the same. He felt better, but he tasted the same to me. Like mine.

Against his mouth, I asked, "We won't be moving too fast if we make love, right?"

"Christ, yes, no…. I don't know, but I do know I don't want to ever screw this up."

"Then take me to your room, Travis Stewart."

He smirked. "I'd be more than happy to." He kissed me again and led me down the hall.

# CHAPTER FOURTEEN

## VIOLET

*W*e made it to his bedroom, slamming into the door as our mouths connected with a new-found fiery fever. God, I'd missed this. Him. How he could make my body react with just a touch, a kiss.

I tore my mouth away to kiss down his neck, then pulled back to tug my tee up and off my body. Travis groaned. He followed my lead, though he actually tore his shirt open, then dropped it to the floor.

He was fitter than his younger self. I licked my lips, wanting to trace the ridges I saw.

"Fuck. Do not look at me like that or it'll be over in five fucking seconds. I know and remember the feel of your pussy, Lettie. I want inside before I come."

Laughing, I undid my jeans and pushed them down while kicking off my shoes. "Then we'd better make it happen."

"Yes," he growled out. "Gloved or ungloved? I'm clean, been checked."

It felt nasty speaking of it, but still, it was good to know because I was on the pill and I wanted to feel all of him inside of me.

"Ungloved. I'm good too and protected." I unhooked my bra and threw it to the side. Cupping my breasts, I squeezed them, rolling my hands over them, then let my fingers glide to my nipples, where I pinched each one.

"Christ," Travis hissed. He undid his jeans, forcing them down his legs. No boxers or briefs were in sight. He kicked them away and stood before me, stroking his large erection.

"God," I moaned, remembering how full I'd felt when he was inside me.

"Remove your panties, Lettie," he ordered. I hooked my thumbs in each side. "Slowly," he clipped. I did. When I stood tall, his eyes were focussed between my legs. I ran a hand down my stomach to touch my mound. His eyes flashed with a hotter heat.

Spreading my legs more, I dipped in a finger and shuddered as it grazed over my already throbbing clit. It'd been years since I was turned on to the point a few quick rubs and I would be coming.

Years because I hadn't had Travis. He was the last man who'd driven me mad with want.

Travis ran out of patience. He came at me, picked me up and threw me down to the bed. He grabbed my legs, hooked them over his shoulders and leaned between them. On the first stroke of his tongue, my back arched off the bed. The second had me gripping the blanket. The third I moaned, and when he sucked and rolled my clit with his tongue and lips, I cried out with the pleasure coursing through my body.

"Trav, babe, please. Need your cock."

He hummed over me, causing my body to twitch. With a kiss, where his tongue entered my hole, he dragged his tongue up to my clit, then nibbled his way up to my mouth. I wrapped him tightly in my arms and kissed him back, hard.

He rocked against me, his cock sliding up and down my pussy, my wetness coating us both. I clamped my knees around his waist, holding him.

As I trailed my lips over his cheek, his chin, his neck, he groaned into my shoulder, all while rocking against me. His dick rubbed sweetly against my clit.

Travis pulled away quickly, grabbed my hips and flipped me over to my stomach. He forced my legs apart and rubbed his hands over my arse before entering me swiftly. I cried out, pain and pleasure mixing and filling my senses.

"Fuck, Lettie," Travis growled into my ear when he leaned over me. "You remember my cock?"

"Yes. God, yes. So big."

"Fills you just right."

Nodding, I hummed, agreeing. He slowly withdrew and slid back in. "Yeah, baby, your pussy was made for me. Just me."

"Yes, Travis. Fuck me."

His leisurely stroke in and out of me wasn't enough.

"Harder, babe," I begged on a moan.

He groaned in the back of his throat. "You've always liked it hard."

"Just from you."

"Yes, Lettie." He reached around, rubbing at my clit, while the other tangled in my hair and pulled me back. I arched. Mewing, panting, and crying out when he fucked me harder and deeper.

His thighs slapped against the back of mine. Travis dropped my hair, wrapped his arm across my chest and brought me close to him. "Fucking mine."

"Yes." I nodded.

He bit my neck, licked it and then bit it again. "Missed this pussy. So damn much." He groaned.

"Missed your cock," I cried.

He pulled out, spun me, and grabbed hold of my legs. I jumped, and he lifted, and I curled my legs around his waist, my hands around his neck. His hand cupped my arse.

"Put me in, Lettie," he growled.

Reaching between us, I held his dick, sliding my hand up and down his length a few times, smirking at his clenched jaw.

"In or I'll spill in your hand."

I didn't want that. Squeezing my legs tighter, I lifted myself, aimed, and sank down on his long, thick, and hard length. I sighed in contentment from the feeling of him filling me.

"Christ, the look you get from having my cock in you... perfection." Using my arse, he guided me off and right back on, hard. I moaned as he did it again and again. His muscles bulging, moving under me. His strength was unbelievable.

"Travis," I whimpered.

"Fuck, yes, say my name again."

I complied. "Travis."

"Yeah, precious, that's who's fucking you. I'm the only one for you from now on."

"God, yes," I panted.

He moved, sitting down on the edge of the bed. When my knees landed on the mattress, I pushed up and then back down. Reaching around, I rested my hands on his knees, lifting up and down, riding his cock like it was made for me, because it was.

Mine. All mine again. Forever.

Travis smoothed his hands over my lower stomach, slid them up until each hand cupped a breast. He played, pinched my nipples, and then leaned in to suck one into his mouth.

"Close," I muttered, lost in the feeling of him inside of me.

"Yes, Lettie. Come on my cock."

"God." I threw my head back just as Travis kissed my neck, sucked my skin between his teeth and bit. I came, crashing, milking, and rocking down on his dick.

His hands slapped down onto my waist, helping me to keep moving. "Lettie," he yelled, swelling and squirting deep inside of me.

When I slumped against him, he laid us down with him still inside of me, as if he didn't want to lose the connection we'd just made, and I was perfectly fine with that. His hand roamed over my arse, my back. God, I'd missed his touch. Having it back was amazing, so much so, tears welled in my eyes.

Clearing my throat, I ignored my emotions and asked, "How long do we have until Izzy gets home?"

"A couple of hours."

I hummed and kissed his shoulder. "I could do that again." Getting to my hands beside his arms, I looked down at him. "Think you can?"

His eyes darkened. "I know I can."

Travis wrapped me in his arms, walking me into the kitchen glued to my back. We both froze. Sitting at the dinner table was someone I didn't expect to see, especially since Travis's property was guarded.

"You wanna fuckin' tell me what the fuck you doin' with my sister?" Talon demanded as he stood, crossing his arms over his chest.

I snorted and went to step forward, but Travis quickly pulled me behind him. I slapped his back. "He's my pain-in-the-arse brother. I'll deal with him."

"No, Vi," Talon said, making his way around the table. "Travis and I gotta sort somethin' out."

"I don't think—"

"Lettie," Travis said softly. Glancing over his shoulder, he shook his head. He looked back to Talon. "I know you hate me—"

"Fuckin' oath."

"But your sister cares for me, and all I can do is promise you I'll never hurt her again."

Talon stopped. His hands fisted down at his sides. He found my eyes over Travis's shoulder. "You want him in your life?"

"Yes," I stated.

"Fuck." He sighed. He looked back to Travis. "You ever cross her in any goddamn way, she won't stop me from huntin' you down and makin' you pay."

Travis nodded. "I wouldn't want it any other way, because if that ever happened, I know I would deserve it."

Talon studied him. He nodded and walked by, hitting his shoulder into Travis's. He stopped in front of me. "Love you, sister."

I thinned my lips, so I didn't cry. "Love you, brother. Even when you're a pain."

He grinned then. "I'll tell Zara you said hey."

"Do that. She doing okay?"

His face softened. Yeah, my brother was completely in love. "Yeah, she's good." He kissed my temple and exited the room.

"Wait," I called. "Travis's people?"

"Unconscious, but alive. Got the brothers watchin' them." He waved over his shoulder and walked out of the house.

"Seems to run in the family," Travis commented.

I turned to him. "What?"

"Knocking out my employees."

That was true. I grinned.

# EPILOGUE

## TRAVIS

*W*aking, I automatically curled Violet closer to me. It had been three months since she took a chance on us, and things were going smoothly. There'd been little things that got her back up, or mine, but we worked through them. Together.

"Morning," I said, kissing her neck.

She stretched. "Morning." Then she shot up to sitting. "It's morning. Shit, Travis, you should have woken me. What happens if Izzy comes in and finds me here?" She slipped out of bed quickly and threw on her jeans and tee. No bra I noticed.

Lying flat with my hands behind my head, I asked, "Don't you think it's time she knows we're together? Something I'm sure she's cottoned on to already."

She spun my way and glared. I smirked in response. Her hands went to her waist. "She wouldn't have cottoned on if you'd stop touching me or kissing my neck and cheek around her."

Chuckling, I climbed out of bed naked. Her hands dropped,

her eyes raking over me, and it was fucking amazing to see them heat from looking at me.

I walked around the bed, pulled her into my arms, and told her, "One day soon we'll have to tell her."

She nodded, leaning back into me. "We will."

I kissed her neck. "Let me get some pants on and I'll see you out."

"All right, but be quick." She turned to slap my arse when I moved off. "I love that arse."

Chuckling, I said, "I know, just like my cock."

She grinned wide. "This is true."

Smiling, I went into the walk-in robe, grabbed a pair of jeans, and slipped them on. My ears picked up a certain sound. I strode into the room just as the bedroom door came flying open.

Violet froze, a look of shock on her face as she stared at a beaming Izzy in the doorway.

"You stayed. Yay, now we can start our girls' day early." She skipped over to Violet, who still seemed in shock and was frozen to the spot. "Can we do my nails first? Then I'll do yours, and after that, we can paint that mud stuff all over our faces. We need to cut up cucumber. Bethany told me she does that with her mum, so we need to, too." She giggled, only to stop and look at me. "Daddy, what's wrong with Lettie?"

Laughing, I walked over, wound my arms around Violet's waist, and gently shook her a little. "Nothing, princess. She's like this every morning without coffee."

"Ah," she muttered, like she understood. "Daddy, is Lettie going to sleep in your room every night now?"

Huh, since Violet was in a state of... I was still going with shock, or it could be panic, I told Izzy, "She sure is."

"Yay. She'll be like my mummy."

Violet hiccupped. I rested my chin on her shoulder and caught her bottom lip trembling.

"Oh no, she really needs coffee, Daddy. Looks like she might cry."

"You could be right, my princess. How about you head down there, grab out the milk and sugar ready for me to make her one."

"I will." She smiled. She turned and skipped out of the room singing some song.

"How are you handling it?"

She sniffed and spun so quickly I had to drop my hands and straighten. Her palms planted to my chest and she shoved me. "You told her I was sleeping here every night."

"Yes." I nodded, smiling.

Then she covered her face with her hands and burst into tears. I wrapped her up again in my arms. "She didn't care I was here. She said I'd be like her mummy. She really likes me."

"No, precious. She loves you, like I do."

"If you ever stop, I'll kick you in the balls."

Chuckling, I told her the truth. "I'll never stop."

She sniffed again, pulled her head up and said, "And *I'll* never stop."

"Stop what?" I asked on a growl.

"Stop loving you, you jackarse."

Grinning, I kissed her.

"Yuck," came from the doorway. "Daddy and Lettie sitting in the tree, K.I.S.S.I.N.G. First comes love, then comes marriage, then comes.... Daddy, how are babies made?"

Coughing, I turned Violet and moved her forward, as if she could protect me from that question. Only she was too busy laughing, probably at my fearful, wide eyes. I quickly told her the first thing that came to my mind. "Come back to me when you're thirty. I'll tell you then."

"Okay." She gave me the thumbs up.

"I thought you were getting out the things for coffee."

"I am, but then I had a question."

"What was it?"

She paused. "I forgot." She giggled. "I'll go get the stuff out so Lettie doesn't cry."

"Thank you," Violet said.

Izzy ran over to her, hugging her tightly. "Anything for you." A second later, she ran out of the room.

Once alone, I asked, "So you're moving in?"

"I don't think I was actually asked, more told." She smiled.

"That was me asking," I offered.

"Then yes, I'd like to move in."

"I guess having you naked in bed is out of the question."

"Travis," she cried. Shaking her head, she made her way to the door. Glancing over her shoulder, she said, "Tonight, when Izzy's in bed, since I'll be staying."

Christ, my chest grew warm. "That you will." She went out the door and I called her back. Her head poked around the edge. "You're my world, Violet."

Her eyes softened. "You're mine too."

VIOLET

I never thought I could be so full of happiness and love, but I was. It had to do with the man in the bedroom and the little girl in the kitchen. Life wouldn't be all perfect for us. There would be times when I wanted to throttle Travis, but I wouldn't change what we had for anything.

They were mine and I was theirs.

Forever.

# ACKNOWLEDGEMENTS

Amanda Berry, this novella wouldn't have happened if it wasn't for your begging. Thank you for wanting Vi and Travis's book so much.

Lindsey Lawson, thank you for everything you do.

To my unwavering, amazing readers, thank you for your help, support, and belief in my stories.

## Chapter 1

With a bloody nose and legs, a split lip and wild tremor going through my body, I picked up the phone and called the one person I knew would help me."Hey, wench, you never call from the house phone... what's wrong?" My best friend's voice had started out happy, then suddenly taken on the edge of panic.

"I-I, Dee, I need your help," I whispered and looked over my shoulder to my passed-out husband on the bed.

On the bed where he had just beaten and raped me.

Yes, we were married; still, no meant no. Cries of pain meant something was wrong. Screaming meant that the one who caused it should stop.

But he didn't.

My husband invaded my body and mind, ruining me in so many ways. I wanted him to pay for what he did. I wanted him to hurt.

But I was scared, and I only saw one way out of it all.

To run.

"I'm coming, Zara," Deanna uttered into the phone and then hung up.

Knowing my husband was so high and drunk that he wouldn't wake, even if the house exploded around him, I started to pack.

Deanna must have heard the urgency in my voice; the journey that would usually take half an hour only took her fifteen minutes. My husband knew nothing of Deanna, and I was glad I'd kept it that way. He hated me having friends; he hated me doing a lot of things, and stupidly I had listened to him at the start. Because back then he was different, he showed me the world and told me that he and I were going to shine through it all.

It took him a year to change, to become his true self, a man I would never have married if I had known how cruel he was. He liked things his way or no way at all.

Deanna came running into the bedroom; I had given her a key months ago, worried something like this would happen. She looked from me to the bed.

"That motherfucker." Her hand went behind her and when she pulled it back around it held a gun.

"No," I cried, my hand going around her wrist as she pointed it at David.

Deanna turned her hard gaze to me. "Look at what he did to you, hun. He—"

"Please, Dee. Please understand I don't want his death on my conscience. He will be more hurt and pissed if we let him be and he wakes finding me gone. I need to get out of here, honey. I need to find a place where he can't find me."

"I want to hurt him, Zara. I want to gut the fucking pig." Tears filled her eyes as she noticed the blood running down my thighs from under my short nightie.

A sob tore through me. "I want to make him pay in the

worst way...and me leaving, escaping him when he thought I couldn't and wouldn't, will be my revenge. Please, please, hun."

"Jesus," she snapped, shaking off my hold on her arm and reaching for my cases. "Are you okay to walk?"

"Y-yes." I sent her a pathetic smile and started for the door. I wouldn't look back. David was now a part of my past, and he deserved nothing from me from that day on. No thought, no tears...nothing.

Deanna was my guiding light. She had been since I met her at the library in our book group. From that night on she was more so. She took me from that house to hers; there she helped me clean up and after we started to make plans.

From her computer I emailed my parents, telling them I was now out from under David's thumb, but I needed time to make sure things would be safe for all of us. I couldn't and wouldn't risk my parents' or brother's lives going back to them. So I moved, with Deanna, to another state. It was there I found out David had left me with last parting gift...I was pregnant. And I would say gift, because when Maya was born my heart couldn't think of her as anything but special. She was my new world and I would do anything to keep her safe.

SIX YEARS LATER

I was enjoying the walk home in the afternoon sun. My boss had an assignment and she kindly gave me the rest of the day off. Maya, my six-year-old, was attending the school sleepover for her grade. So I picked myself up some chocolate, a DVD, a bottle of wine, and Chinese takeout for dinner. Even better, my best friend, Deanna was coming over later to help me make the most of my relaxing night in.

I rounded the corner to my street and froze. My annoying, but hot neighbour was standing out the front of my other neighbour's house talking to the Campbells' nineteen-year-old daughter, Karen. I hung my head, ready to stride past, humming a tune along the way to cover their voices. Still, her high cackle broke through, as irritating as always. I was close to freedom and just past them, deafening myself with my out-of-tune hum when someone grabbed my arm and spun me back around.

"Kitten," Talon said.

My eyes closed of their own accord to cherish the sound. It happened every time I heard his deep grumble of a voice.

"Uh, what? Oh, Talon?" I blushed and bit my bottom lip.

He laughed. "I asked where Maya was."

"Oh, um, she's at school. Her class is having a sleepover," I informed him. Though I didn't know why.

"Right. So…." he began but stopped to look into my shopping bags. "We're watching *27 Dresses*, eating Chinese, and drinking wine. Sounds like a plan. What time do you want me to come over? I could bring dessert." He grinned mischievously.

I looked around him to Karen. She huffed something and stomped off. I then turned my gaze back to the hunk with his messy, needs-a-cut black hair and dark brown eyes.

I'd never forgotten the day I moved onto the street and into my three-bedroom weatherboard home two years ago and learned that I was living across the road from the local biker compound, with their head honcho right next door to me. I had just moved with Maya out of Deanna's house after being there for four years. I was feeling frightened and overwhelmed, as well as a little inebriated after having a few welcome-to-the-new-house drinks with Deanna. Deanna left and I was in bed, but Maya kept waking up from the loud music being played next door. After she drifted back to sleep for the third time, I went—armed with the confidence of the alcohol—next door, dressed in my pink nightie with a kitten on the front and combat boots. I banged on the door. A short, hairy guy opened it and raised his eyebrows at me.

"Who is the freaking owner of this place?" I demanded.

"Yo, boss," the man called over his shoulder.

And I swear my heart stopped when Talon walked his broad, muscular form my way dressed in jeans and a white tee with a leather vest hanging open over it. Everything but him faded into the background.

"Whadup, cupcake?" He leaned against the doorframe and crossed his arms over his chest.

My eyes closed. Until I remembered, I was there for a reason, and that reason was more important than Mr Hotness.

Upon opening them, I went straight into a glare that could scare most young children. His mouth twitched. "I just moved in next door. I thought 'wow, what a nice place to start anew! That was until your bloody stupid music started blasting on a freakin' Monday night. I have a daughter who is starting her new school tomorrow." I stepped up closer. "Turn down the music. *Now*," I hissed.

"Wow, boss, you have a fuckin' wildcat living next door," someone said from behind him. Manly chuckles began. I ignored the others and kept my glare on bossman.

"More like a wild kitten." He smiled, looking down at my nightie. "Don't worry, kitten. I'll turn down the music. But, it'll cost you."

I blanched and stepped back, all confidence gone. "Wh...what?"

The men laughed louder.

"Just one kiss, babe."

"Talon!" A woman growled from somewhere behind the laughing crowd.

"You're a... pig," I said and walked away. Not long after that, the music was turned down.

From that day on, no matter how many times I tried to dodge Talon Marcus, I still managed to bump into him and make a fool of myself—something that he greatly enjoyed. I could tell from his small teasing smirks or laughter at my expense because he knew what he did to me and my libido. He enjoyed playing games with me... and okay, sometimes I even enjoyed them, deep, deep down. Because every time something happened, he made me feel desired.

However, feeling *that* scared me, and in turn, caused me to become a chicken, so to avoid the man who invaded my dreams I spent a lot of time with my daughter at Deanna's.

An example of why I had to steer clear of such hotness was what happened four days ago. Maya was at Deanna's while I quickly ran home to do a few errands and clean the house without my daughter making more of a mess. I had just gotten out of my car when Talon magically appeared out of nowhere.

"Kitten." He smiled.

Upon opening my eyes, I squeaked, "Talon," and tried to walk around him. He wouldn't have it of course and stepped in front of me.

"What are you doin' tonight?" he asked, and I watched as his hands slowly rose to tuck my long wavy hair behind my shoulder. My eyes stayed glued to his hand as his fingers gently ran down my arm to my hand. There his fingers wrapped around mine and tugged.

"Kitten," he chuckled.

Shaking my head, I looked up and glared at the bad, bad biker man.

God, he loved playing with me.

Still, even though my body loved to be played with, I was no longer that woman.

The woman who risked.

And it was a guess, but I was sure it was a good guess that Talon Marcus, president of the Hawks Motorcycle Club, was one huge risk to my heart.

"I'm,"—I licked my dry lips, my eyes widening when his beautiful eyes watched my tongue—"I'm busy, um, it was, ah, really nice to see you, Talon, but I have to go," I blurted, and then to my... disgrace, practically ran to my front door with his deep chuckle following me.

As soon as I was inside my door, I closed it quickly and leaned against it, my breathing erratic. In the last six months I had frequently seen Talon popping up out of nowhere wanting to talk to me, to ask me what my plans were, and every time I acted like a freaked-out teen whose boy crush had just spoken to her.

No matter how my body wanted to jump his bones and get jiggy with him, my mind stayed strong and reminded myself that a relationship came with too much trouble.

At least that was what I kept telling myself.

"Zara?"

I blinked back into the now and answered, "I—ah. No, I don't think. I mean, I'm not good company, and I have a friend coming over—"

"That's fine, just means we'll have to be quick." He winked.

Rolling my eyes, I walked off, but not before he slapped me on the behind and then strode past me laughing.

I grumbled under my breath all the way up the steps, ignoring the other bikers across the road at the compound laughing, yet again, at me.

Two hours later, I'd had a bath and gotten into my pink-with-black-kittens flannel PJs. Deanna texted an hour ago saying, *Hey, twat head. Not sure if I can make it. I'll let you know.*

So I sat down at my small, four-seater wooden table by the kitchen's large bay windows to eat my reheated Chinese. I had always found that Chinese tasted better when reheated.

Only then the doorbell sang. *Maybe Deanna made it after all.* I walked through my small lounge, which was furnished with a floral couch and one chair. A television sat on a long black unit against the wall, and a wooden chest acted as a coffee table in the centre. Nothing matched and that was the way I liked it. I'd saved and bought all of it myself, so I loved every piece of furniture in my house. I smiled before opening the front door.

"Kitten," Talon said as he looked at me from top to bottom. With a grin, he moved fast, because the next thing I knew, he was kissing me. My eyes sprang wide when his hot mouth touched mine.

"Talon," I mumbled around his lips, trying to shove him back. Unfortunately, well, not really, but still, yes unfortunately, when I spoke it gave Talon's tongue the chance to sneak in. As soon as it hit mine, I melted on a moan of abso-freakin'-lute pleasure. My abdomen clenched and my nether region quivered. I wrapped my arms around his neck and gave back as good as I was getting. In return, I received a groan. He picked me up, stepped inside, and kicked the front door closed behind him.

*Holy crap, Talon's kissing me. ME. God, he is good. Wait, why is he kissing me? ME?*

"Hot damn. I need some popcorn for this," I heard my best friend say.

I pulled away. My arms dropped to my sides, and he let me

take a step back. Both of us were breathing hard. I took another step back, looked over Talon's shoulder, and found Deanna, smiling hugely, standing in the doorway with her hand still on the doorknob.

"Girl, you said he was fine, but you didn't say he was fucking F.I.N.E."

Talon raised his eyebrows at me and turned to face Deanna, in all his tight jeans and white tee glory.

"I-I've never said anything," I muttered.

"Hey, Talon. I'm Deanna, Zara's best mate. I've been waiting for a glance of you for two fucking years. Oh, and I'm the one who will whip out some whoop-ass on you if you fuck her over, biker dude or not," she said in a pleasant tone, and then smiled sweetly.

Talon surprisingly didn't laugh. He looked her over and looked back at me. I knew what was running through his mind. Deanna and I were complete opposites. I was on the short side, had curves and lightly tanned skin from my Mexican background. I was sure Talon had the same sort of mix in his blood, only his skin was a little more like cocoa with a dollop of milk.

I had long, wavy, dark brown hair, and dark, forest-green eyes. Deanna was tall, thin, and was lucky enough to have been bestowed with a great rack. She had blonde hair, sky-blue eyes, and freckles on her nose to make her look that much cuter. She also had a big case of attitude. Though, it was all a front, of course. We'd both been through our own personal hell. We were just lucky to have found each other at the end.

"Nice to meet you, Deanna, and you have nothing to worry about," Talon replied.

*What does that mean?*

Deanna glared at him for a moment and then smiled. I felt, for a second, a pang of jealousy. Her smile had been the end of many men over the years, and right now, in her black pants and hugging tee that read 'watch 'em bounce' she looked great.

"I better not. Alrighty, wait till I get some popcorn and you two can continue what you were doing." She clapped her hands together.

"Uh, no. We can't. That—nuh-uh,"—I shook my head —"shouldn't have happened." My mind was in a whirl of thoughts.

Talon turned to me and said calmly, "It's been a hell of a long time coming."

"Wh-what?" I shook my head again.

"Come on, Zara, give the shmuck a chance. Then at least if it doesn't work out, I get to kick his bad-boy biker arse. A cute one at that; right again, lovey." She nodded at me.

I glared at my *ex*-best friend. "I have never said anything about his behind. Deanna, a word in the kitchen." I gestured with my head. Then I looked at Talon. "Uh, maybe you should go."

"I think I'll stay, kitten." He grinned and made his way to the couch. He sat down and propped his feet up on my chest— the wooden one—and turned on the TV.

I pulled the smiling Deanna down the hall, into my bedroom, and closed the door. Then I frantically got changed into jeans and a tee. Talon had already seen me in my PJs once, and that was once too many.

I spun to Deanna, put my hands on my hips, and glowered at her as she sat on my bed grinning.

"Oh, don't start. You need to live a little, girl. And I think biker boy can help you along the way."

"Deanna," I hissed. "I see nothing but danger with him around; and for God's sake, I am nowhere near his type. Look at me," I said, waving my hands up and down my body.

"And?" Deanna asked while looking at me like I was a loon.

"I have hips, I have a pudding belly, and I have dark brown hair. Not blonde and skinny, like he's always with, and have seen leave his place, and... Jesus, what the hell am I explaining myself for? There's danger all around him. Danger, Deanna. I can't go back to that. You'd have a better chance with him. Not that I want one."

She ignored my last statement. "You sound like that fucked-up robot off... shit, what's that show you like?"

"*Lost in Space.*"

"That's it." She took a deep breath. "Zee, hun, you don't know that. Sure he's a badarse, but he ain't nothing like that other jerk-off. Nothing."

I threw my hands up in the air. "*You* don't know that. I have to think of Maya. She's my number-one priority."

"What about you, though? When will you let yourself be happy?"

"I'll wait till Maya's twenty. Then I can think about myself," I said, and crossed my arms over my chest.

"I bet—" Deanna was cut off by a knock on the front door.

I looked at Deanna and raised my eyebrows. I didn't know why, maybe I thought she magically knew who was at the front door. She shrugged, and then we both heard Talon growl, "Who the fuck are you?"

We bolted from my bedroom and ran down the hall. Coming into the living room, I focused on who was at the front door.

*Oh, hell.*

"Um, hi, Michael." I waved over Talon's shoulder because he hadn't moved from the doorway. He still held the door with one hand, as if he were ready to shut it on Maya's teacher from last year's face.

"Hi, Zara." Michael smiled.

"What are you doing here?" I asked, and tried to open the

door wider to get it from Talon's grip. But he wouldn't budge, so I gave up.

Michael produced a bunch of wildflowers from behind his back. "I saw these and thought of you."

"She doesn't want them," Talon said.

"Talon!" I scolded.

"And who are you?" Michael asked.

"Her man."

I coughed and sputtered. "Ah, no you're not."

"Hot damn," I heard in the background from Deanna.

"Yes. I am." He turned to me, his form blocking my view of outside and Michael.

I put my hands on my hips. "Since when?" I glared.

"Kitten." He smiled. "Since I stuck my tongue down your throat and you curled your body around mine, moaning for more."

I was sure my eyes popped out of my head and walked off, then skipped with my heart down the path.

"Hot-double-damn!" Deanna laughed. "You'll have to give her a minute. Sorry, Mike. I think you're about ten seconds too late."

Talon shut the door in his face, which broke me out of my trance.

"Goddamn it, Talon. That was rude. And I am not your woman!" I opened the door and stomped down the front steps after a retreating Michael.

"Michael, I'm so sorry about that Neanderthal. That was very sweet of you to bring me flowers." Though, I didn't understand why since I'd told him "no" fifty times already when he'd asked me out.

"Don't ever do it again," Talon warned from the front porch.

I glared up at him. He winked and smiled down at me.

"I can see I've come at the wrong time. Maybe I should come back?" Michael asked.

"Uh…" was my response.

"No," came from Talon.

"I wouldn't bother," from Deanna.

I turned to them and sliced across my neck with my finger. Really, I was prepared to kill the both of them.

Spinning back to Michael, I smiled. "I'm sorry, Michael, but right now, at this time, I'm not ready for anything—"

A scoff came from Talon.

I continued, "The thought was very sweet, and I think you're a great guy—" God, I hated doing this; I always felt bad. Especially with a guy who was still holding flowers for me. "And you never know, maybe in the future—"

"Try never," Talon growled.

"Ever." Deanna giggled.

I winced. What was with the running commentary from the loco-train people? "Sorry, Michael."

"That's okay, Zara. I'll come back in a couple of weeks, see how things are."

I stopped myself from rolling my eyes. *Is that the future?*

"You come back, I'll kill you." Talon started moving from the front porch toward us. I quickly ushered Michael out the front gate and closed it.

"Everything okay, boss?" Griz asked. Griz was short for Grizzly, his biker nickname because he was built like a bear, in a cuddly sort of way. Not that he had a belly; he didn't. He was just tall, with very wide shoulders, arms, and legs. Griz was stalking across the street toward us. Two others, whom I hadn't met, were standing on the other side of the road, legs apart, arms folded across their chests, looking menacing. I'd only met Griz because he helped me one day when I was attacking my lawn mower with a sledgehammer when it wouldn't start. He'd jogged across with an amused expression and asked, "Can I help, lady?" I let him, of course, or I'd be in jail right now for murder. I would have found a gun somehow.

I saw Michael studying Griz who was in his full motorcycle ensemble, including his black leather vest with a Hawks patch sewn onto it, their club's name.

"Y-y-you're a member of Hawks," Michael stuttered.

Griz stopped beside Michael and stared down at him. "Yeah, what of it?" he snapped.

"N-nothing." Michael turned back to Talon. "He, he called you 'boss.'"

Talon grinned his wicked grin and I grabbed the fence for support as Talon said, "Heard that, did ya?"

"Um." He looked to the ground. "Zara, I don't think I'll be back. Bye." He quickly marched off to his car. I was surprised his car didn't fly off, squealing down the road.

Deanna burst out laughing and walked toward us.

I sighed and ignored Talon's presence beside me. Instead, I turned my attention to Griz. "Hi, Griz. How's things?" He looked from me to Talon and then back.

"Great, Wildcat, and you?" He smirked. Wildcat had become my nickname from all the bikers since that first night. For some strange reason, no one else was allowed to call me kitten except Talon.

"Fine." I rolled my eyes and watched as the other two bikers disappeared into the compound.

"Now that's what I call entertaining. Girl, I gotta come to your house more often." Deanna grinned.

"Deanna, I think from now on I'm going to be a regular visitor at *your* place." *Just like I have been.*

"Kitten—" Talon began with a tone of warning.

"Pfft. Don't you 'kitten' me," I said with my back to him. He slipped his arms around my waist and pulled me close against his front. I held off a sigh of pleasure and tried to move away. It was impossible. I looked over my shoulder at him and bit my tongue to hold the moan. He looked gorgeous, even though his eyes told me he was annoyed. Still, they were laced with a little bit of lust as well.

Griz laughed but covered it with a cough when Talon glared at him.

"Oh, girly, we need to celebrate this. Let's get drunk," Deanna said. "Lord knows I need it."

I doubted I was supposed to hear that. I looked over at her and knew she was hiding something from me, but what was the mystery?

"And what are we celebrating exactly?"

"You and Talon gettin' it on." She gave me the *duh* look.

I went to move again but didn't get anywhere. "Uh, no. There is no Talon and Zara."

"Uh-huh." She smiled and looked at us from top to bottom. Okay, so to some it could seem different. Because I may have relaxed against Talon's warm, hot weight and my arms may be... okay, were resting on top of his, which were still wrapped around my waist.

*Holy crap, I'm in Talon's arms.*

He moved an arm from around me and swept my hair aside, then kissed my neck, which involuntarily arched so he could have better access.

*Holy cow, Talon's kissing my neck. In front of people.*

That didn't help my side of things. I nudged his head away with my own, and with some force, wiggled my way from his —wanted...so much needed...No!—unwanted and unneeded comfort.

I made my escape to Deanna's side.

*Oh, my God, is my breathing heavy again? Yes, yes it is. Damn him and his sinful body.*

"You"—I pointed my finger at him and glared—"stay over there. This"—I gestured between the two of us—"can't happen."

Deanna scoffed. Griz laughed.

"Kitten, I know you want me. Your body doesn't lie. It's only a matter of time before I'll be in your pants..." He trailed off as Griz's phone rang.

Griz flipped it open. "Yo? Yep." He closed it and looked at Talon. "Business, boss. Later, ladies."

"Bye, Griz." I smiled. It wasn't his fault his boss was a chauvinist arse-hat.

"See ya, hot stuff," Deanna purred, causing Griz to look over his shoulder, confused. He didn't understand that Deanna was attracted to older men, and Griz was definitely older. Deanna and I both sat at twenty-six. My guess, Talon was mid-to-late thirties, and Griz, with his long, muddy-brown-with-grey hair, and hard-aged eyes seemed to be hitting early forties.

"Kitten, I have to go. But if you two are having drinks, why don't you come by the compound later. I'll have a couple with you." With that, he grabbed my chin, kissed me hard and quickly, before my knee had the chance to hit his groin, and left.

Of course, I watched his fine arse walk away, and I was sure he knew it.

"Yeah, you keep fighting that, hun." Deanna laughed and walked into the house.

# ALSO BY LILA ROSE

**Hawks MC: Ballarat Charter**

Holding Out (FREE) Zara and Talon

Climbing Out: Griz and Deanna

Finding Out (novella) Killer and Ivy

Black Out: Blue and Clarinda

No Way Out: Stoke and Malinda

Coming Out (novella) Mattie and Julia

**Hawks MC: Caroline Springs Charter**

The Secret's Out: Pick, Billy and Josie

Hiding Out: Dodge and Willow

Down and Out: Dive and Mena

Living Without: Vicious and Nary

Walkout (novella) Dallas and Melissa

Hear Me Out: Beast and Knife

Breakout (novella) Handle and Della

Fallout: Fang and Poppy

**Standalones related to the Hawks MC**

Out of the Blue (Lan, Easton, and Parker's story)

Out Gamed (novella) (Nancy and Gamer's story)

Outplayed (novella) (Violet and Travis's story)

**Romantic comedies**

Making Changes

Making Sense

Fumbled Love

**Trinity Love Series**
Left to Chance
Love of Liberty (novella)

**Paranormal**
Death (with Justine Littleton)
In The Dark

## CONNECT WITH LILA ROSE

**Webpage**: www.lilarosebooks.com

**Facebook**: http://bit.ly/2du0taO

**Instagram**: www.instagram.com/lilarose78/

**Goodreads:**

www.goodreads.com/author/show/7236200.Lila_Rose

CPSIA information can be obtained
at www.ICGtesting.com
Printed in the USA
BVHW052233221222
654900BV00007B/82